Love's Journey Home

The Search for Love

C. A. SIMONSON

Cover Design by C.A. Simonson and publicdomainpictures.com
All scripture quotations are taken from the Holy Bible
King James version, public domain.
Amazing Grace by John Newton, 1772 – public domain

Published by Aspen Run Press

Copyright © 2013 C.A. Simonson
All rights reserved.
ISBN: 1492995118
ISBN-13: 978-1492995111

DEDICATION

This book is a memory to our family's legacy.
Names, characters, places, and incidents are used
fictitiously, though based on true events
of men in my life.
Men who through great adventures experienced life
first-hand. This is the legacy of grandfathers, fathers,
husband, and sons.
To these men,
I dedicate this book.

Table of Contents

ACKNOWLEDGMENTS

I am grateful to my husband who has been patient through the writing of this book. He had been a listening ear, help with reading and re-reading the manuscript and a springboard of ideas and suggestions for many of the actual happenings in this book.

Thank you to friends and colleagues at the Writers Guild of Springfield, MO who spurred me on to finish this task and gave encouragement and critique along the way.

1 Going Back

Going back to my home town of Tekamah, Nebraska filled me with trepidation. It had been almost ten years since I last saw my brother and sisters, but it seemed like an eternity. Would I ever find them? Would anyone remember me, or them? Not sure why I let myself be talked into going back; it was a crazy, miserable, strange time of my life. Much I wanted to forget. But I had to go back one more time. Had to see if anyone knew anything about my family.

I drove through the town as slow as the limit allowed; maybe I would spot someone I knew. The old town hadn't changed much. The one room schoolhouse which also served as a church was now a museum. The doc's office became a small clinic. From town, I headed west along Old Tree Lane where tall cottonwoods guarded either side of the road. Brisk fall winds persuaded the trees to powder the ground with fluffy white puffs of cotton. Past Mill Pond, the stately Johnson homestead still guarded its place on the corner. I recalled with sadness the death of my two brothers while in the Johnsons' care. Turning the car north, I passed the Wheeler farm where I grew from a boy to a man. It looked empty. Made me think with fondness of old Mac and wondered if he or his missus were still alive.

Almost at the old homestead, I slowed with the thought of turning around. Why did I come back? The memories were way too painful, but I had to know. I took a deep breath and drove up the road toward home. When I spotted the old rickety wooden fence surrounding the abandoned shack, the memories washed back with a flood of debris.

There we were – seven of us – perched atop that splintery wooden fence waiting for Pa to come back. Darkness started to settle in and with it a slight drizzle. The wind picked up steam, howling loudly as it screeched around the barn. I shivered and wrapped my arms inside my coat to keep warm. I looked down the row on my brothers and sisters; saw Gracie whimpering again. She looked so pitiful and scared. None of us dared move off the fence. Pa had said to sit here until he came back and he meant it. He was a mean man to deal with when he got drunk. I shivered again as I remembered him locking the shack, staggering towards the truck and driving away without a look back. We were all afraid of what Pa would do if he came back and caught us away from our fence post.

"Where *is* he?" whispered Mikey.

"Ah's gittin' cold," sobbed Josie.

I was worried too. When Pa left, he was already half-drunk. Sadly, Pa loved his drink. He took to drinking more since Mama left. As long as I'd known, he was always a drinker. One time, he came home so drunk, he acted crazy and out of his mind like a wild man. He started to beat Mama. He slapped her face so hard, she stumbled and fell to the floor.

"Where's my dinna'?" he hollered. The table was set; Mama made us all wait for him to come home, but he wasn't satisfied. He grabbed the tablecloth and yanked the whole thing to the floor with one swoop, breaking every dish. Mama stood there wide-eyed and scared. Her body shook as she dodged another drunken swing from his hand. He staggered towards Dolly with a raised fist, and that was more than Mama could handle. I saw her eyes flare with anger. She grabbed the baby and put herself between Dolly and the madman she called her husband. "Get outside quick!" she ordered. She pushed us out the door, and slammed it behind her. All we could do is leave – fast. Mama and four children marched down the dark country road walking and waiting until Pa passed out on the bed in a drunken stupor. When we thought it was safe, we would tiptoe into the house.

On that freezing cold night so long ago, all he said was, "Git yore stuff on! Ah'm goin' ta town. Ya'll git on that fence and wait there 'til I gits back; an' don' ya dare move an inch!"

His breath reeked of liquor. Gracie was too small to balance atop of the wooden fence post, so Pa just "hung" her there by her coat so she wouldn't fall off. I wasn't sure what to think or do. All I knew was that it was getting colder by the minute. So, we waited; thought he was probably in town drinking some more and would be even meaner when he came back. I shivered again when I remembered he locked the door. We couldn't even get back in the shack. What was he thinking?

C.A. SIMONSON

2 Fence Sittin'

It had only been a few weeks since Mama left us. Pa had lined us up on the fence that night too. It was an awful night. One by one, he made us perch on our post. The shack was way too crowded as it was. Guess he figured the kids wouldn't be in Mama's way when she gave birth if we were outside on the fence. He was really nervous that night. I could tell by the way he chewed on his mustache and paced the floor.

"Now, jes' set out here a spell," he ordered. "Soon ya'll have yorsef a new brotha' or sista'! I'll come an' tell ya's; then ya'll kin come back in. I'm gonna go find someone to help yer Ma now."

He went into town to find someone to come help Mama deliver the baby. I hoped Pa would hurry. I knew something was wrong – dreadfully wrong as we listened to Mama's screams and pitiful cries of pain. But we were told to sit on the fence and wait – wait until we were told we could go inside. So we sat and waited and talked and played games and thought. Besides, if we were loud enough, we wouldn't hear Mama's cries. Fence-sitting gave us lots of time to think.

I was the third born of seven. Big brother Guy was the oldest, soon to be fourteen; Dolly was twelve. I sat next in line, then Mikey, my best bud, sat on the other side of me. He was nine. Past Mikey sat the twins, Jesse and Josie, age six, and then baby Gracie, who couldn't perch herself on the fence. She was only four.

I was named after my great-grandfather Timothy Franklin, but everyone called me Frankie. I was almost ten and a half.

Guy was the thinker, the take-charge sort of guy. He was strong as an ox, and almost as big. He was smart, too. We all looked up to him when we needed help. I admired Guy a lot and wanted to be just like him. My older sister Dolly was quiet and pretty, slender and tall like Mama. She had Mama's eyes, the color of a clear blue sky and Mama's silky blond Norwegian hair. Dolly was a hard worker too; she had to be in order to help Mama with all the other children. I was born a few years before the Great Depression. Mama always said I was so independent because I was born on Independence Day, July 4, 1926. My best bud and younger brother Mikey came along two years later. Things started to get very crowded in the little shanty we lived in. We learned to live, eat and sleep in cramped quarters and make the best of it – or hear the worst of it.

The twins, Jesse and Josie, were nothing alike – in looks or personalities. Josie was quiet and shy; she wouldn't hurt a fly. Jesse, on the other hand, liked to think he could do anything at anytime, anywhere. He was loud and proud of it. Truth was, most of the time he was just a loud-mouth boaster. He wasn't as brave as he let on; he really needed his twin sister to balance him. Mikey and I teased the daylights out of Jesse and the little girls, but we wouldn't dare cross Guy, and well, Dolly was just too nice. Besides, she would tell Mama.

Jesse made a good target more times than not. He loved cold tea with lots of sugar. So one time Mikey and I got the idea to put salt in his tea instead. We changed the sugar for salt in the bowl, and invited Jesse to have a nice glass of cold tea. Jesse put one teaspoonful after another in his glass. Mikey looked at me cross-eyed, and I almost doubled over to hold back a giggle. Chuckled to myself as I thought of it all over again. Jesse only took one drink – but it was a huge gulp – and spurted it back out in an instant – all over the floor. Mikey and I ducked out the door, but Mama knew what happened. She wasn't too happy with us, but we laughed until we cried as we watched Jesse sputter and spit all over the floor. He didn't get over that one for a long time.

My daydreaming on the fence was interrupted as Jesse coughed again and poor little Gracie let out another whimper. She was the youngest. Now she shivered; her tiny body shook as the wind assaulted her. She had the saddest look on her face, and dared herself not to cry. I was real worried about her. I tried not to think about it, but it wasn't working. I could still hear her small shaky sobs through the howl of the wind. We had to get her off this fence post into some warmth.

Why wouldn't he let us stay inside out of the wind? Why did he lock us out? Anything would be warmer than out here. Pa told us to sit tight until he came back, and we all knew we'd get paddled or more if we moved too far away from our assigned posts.

The old shack had been a great deal, or so Pa thought. It was small, but at least it had three bedrooms plus a barn out back. Even had fencing already made for the animals he hoped to raise someday. We all looked forward to our own room with a real bed to sleep on. The lean-to only had one bedroom, and that had been Mama's and Pa's. Guy,

Dolly and I had to sleep on the floor. But even the new shack became small when more kids came along. I think that's when the fence-sitting started; every time Mama had another baby, we ended up waiting on our wooden post.

The rickety fence crawled its crooked path around our small acre of property – not too high that animals or kids couldn't jump over; it was just a property marker. Broken in places, the logs that had slipped out of their sockets lay rotting on the ground. There was one good stretch of seven or eight posts in back of the house where it seemed we ended up whenever we were not allowed in the house.

And that last night? Well, Pa was too drunk to know what he was doing. He wasn't thinking too straight when he left. He just locked up the place and told us to sit on the fence and wait. We knew we best obey or suffer the consequences from a drunken lunatic. He usually came back after a couple hours. Truth was, Pa never did come back that night.

3 Best Buds

Telling stories was a good pastime as we sat waiting. Helped the time go faster, it seemed. Reminded me of other times we perched on an old fence.

"Hey Mikey!" I yelled his way. "Remember those pigs we used to watch roll in the mud? They were so funny!"

"Yeah, Frankie," he laughed. "We even named 'em. Ol' Joe was the meanest, I think."

"Remember that day we rode Ol' Joe?"

"Whew!" Mikey let out a whistle, "still got a scar on my left leg 'cuz of Ol' Joe!"

Pa could never quite decide what to do for a living. First it was chickens, then cows. The summer before, Pa figured he would breed pigs. The wooden fence behind the shack was already there to house the pigs. It got pretty muddy in that pen, but the pigs loved it. The pig idea did better for Pa than the cows. He tried to raise cows during the summer of the big drought – the big Dust Bowl, some called it. Our family was too large and too poor to afford feed. When the watering holes dried up and no grass was left in the fields, the cows died of starvation. The pig-raising idea didn't last long either, but we enjoyed them while they were there.

I chuckled again remembering the day Mikey and I sat on the fence and watched Ol' Joe, the fat pig, and

Gus, the spotted pig, run around and around the pen. I shook my head as I remembered the crazy antics of that day. We were lucky to be alive.

"Mikey! 'Member how I said, 'Jump off the fence and see if you can catch Ol' Joe?'"

"See if you can jump on Ol' Joe!" Mikey corrected. "And I waited and waited until Ol' Joe was closest to the fence and then I took a dive right onto that mean old pig! It squealed like I'd poked him with a stick! I about lost my balance when he jerked sideways and took off running around the pen," Mikey laughed.

"Ol' Joe didn't like his rider too well, huh, Mikey? He kept bumping the fence trying to knock you off. It wasn't long before you were in the mud."

"Yeah, but I got back on. I wasn't afraid like you!" Mikey teased.

"I wasn't afraid! It just took me a while to get on," I defended.

I had waited for Ol' Joe to come back around, but the hog eyed me with suspicion. I threw down a corn cob to bait the spotted pig we called Gus. He was almost as big as Ol' Joe, only a little slower. Gus saw the cob and started towards it.

"We both rode, remember? I jumped on Gus and grabbed his ears and you got back on Ol' Joe. We raced round and round the pen! Those pigs tried their best to bump us against the fence to knock us off. Never heard such squealing and oinking going on in my life!"

We laughed as we thought about fun times. I shifted my weight to the other leg so it wouldn't go to sleep and scooted up a little more.

"I thought you were a goner that day, Mikey."

"Yeah, me too. Our fun ride became scary in a hurry when angry Ol' Joe smashed my leg against the fence. It scraped up my leg pretty good, and knocked me right into the mud hole."

"I saw right away that your jeans were bloody and I knew that pig had hurt you bad. Ol' Joe saw the blood too. The mean stare in his eye looked like he was headed for the kill. He was one mean old pig. It was lucky you fell into that mud hole. The mud stopped the bleeding a little, but not enough; the other pigs already had scent of the blood. They all ran straight towards you!" I shook my head at the gruesome memory.

"I'm glad you were there for me Frankie. You are always there for me! 'Member how fast you hopped off Gus and ran over to me?" Mikey hopped off his fence post to demonstrate, ran over by me, then picked up some mud as he spoke and threw it over the fence. "I was still in the mud hole; couldn't move my leg. You picked up handfuls of mud and slung it at the other pigs trying to surround me. 'Let's get you outta here Mikey,' you told me, 'cuz those pigs will bite you good!'"

"Yeah, I wasn't sure that was true, but that's what Pa told us. Didn't he say they would eat us? I watched the pigs get madder by the minute. I'll admit it. I was scared. I pulled you up by the sleeve and told you to move fast!

Mikey chuckled again and hopped on the fence rail beside me. "I screamed pretty loud 'cuz my leg hurt mighty bad, and you just kept pulling me, dragging me to the fence."

"I had to get you out of the way before Ol' Joe took a chomp out of your foot. If only Mama hadn't seen us."

"Something made her glance out the back window. She saw us hurrying to get out of the pigpen and onto the fence."

"She met us at the door and she didn't smile at all, did she?" I chuckled.

"'Boys, ya'll go out back and pick yoreselves a good slender twig from the willer tree.' That's what she said. She didn't look mad or nothing, but she sure didn't smile either."

"Yep. Little did we know what we were in for, huh, Mikey?"

"Yeah, you got that right. Our bottoms weren't ready to ride those pigs again for a real long time after our meeting with the willow sticks!"

"Yeah. After the time I stuck the pie tin in my backside and Mama hurt her hand, she found the willow sticks made a bigger sting on our legs."

We fell quiet again, thinking about past events. I patted my brother on the back. Just two years apart in age, Mikey was my best bud. I was thankful for my brother. Mikey was also the accident-prone kid in the family. If there was an accident going to happen, it would probably happen to him. If he didn't bump his head on the cupboard occasionally, he fell down or got a stick poked in his eye. He smashed his finger in the door once and almost took it off. Still has a strange-looking mashed-up finger to this day.

Mikey and I did everything together. There were woods out back to hunt and a little pond down the road for some great bullhead fishing. The hill on the back dirt road was great to slide down in the winter.

We even dug a fort in the woods for our hideout when we played cowboys and Indians.

The fort, our hole in the ground covered with brush, was the result of digging for treasure. We overheard Pa telling a story about a bum burying something in the woods, and we just knew it had to be hidden treasure. Mikey and I found a spot we thought would be the perfect hiding place for a treasure and dug down so deep we could almost stand up in the hole. That's when we struck something hard. We were so excited! We thought we struck a treasure chest full of gold.

"We found it, Frankie!" Mikey shrieked. "It's gotta be the treasure chest!"

We dug some more and kept hitting the hard object. We brushed away the dirt as fast as our hands would allow, and attempted to unearth the solid object beneath our shovels. It was flat and hard, a kind of dark grey color. The more dirt that was brushed away, we realized our treasure wasn't a gold-filled chest; it was just a plain old flat rock.

I looked at Mikey with an "I-told-you-so" look as our enthusiasm faded.

"Oh well," mused my always-objective brother, "at least we can really hide in our new fort now."

"Leave it to you, Mikey. Who cares if we didn't find the treasure? You are right. We have a special place all to ourselves. Bet we can even bring some blankets out here. We have a solid rock floor now. It will make a good, cool hideout. This will be our secret place."

"Yeah," Mikey agreed. "Good idea, Frankie! Let's get some pine branches and cover it up, so no one sees it."

Mikey loved secrets. In the next few weeks, we gathered loose boards to put on top of our hideout, and then covered it with the pine branches. The best part was that no one knew about it except for Mikey and me. We stored flashlights and some jerky, apples, and crackers for snacks. Logs became stools. It was a great get-away, nice and cool on those hot summer days. We loved to camp out.

There were so many adventures to find in the woods. It was our second home in the summer. We often spent all day with our BB guns hunting birds, squirrels, or chipmunks, and no one thought to look for us. Mama knew we were safe, and besides she had her chores and too many other kids to care for. She never worried. She knew we'd come home if we got hungry enough. Pa figured we were too young to do the hard chores, and he had Guy to help him, so he didn't care where we were either, as long as we kept out of his hair.

It was a game, you know, sitting on the fence. We made it be. Our fence-sitting stories just helped pass the time. Pa would be back soon. He promised, and most of the time, he kept his promises. So we played our games and told our stories while we waited and wondered where he was.

4 New Baby

Whether it was waiting for a calf to be born, watching

pigs, or waiting on a new baby, we played our fence games until Pa came to tell us it was time to come in. We tried to see who could stay on the fence the longest, who could sit the straightest, who could balance with one leg and arm out straight, or lean back the farthest. Jesse, the youngest boy, was the first to fall off, but would never admit he was the weakest. He bragged he could stay on the longest, then blame his fall on his leg going to sleep or some other cockamamie excuse. Truth was, he had no balance. The same was true that awful night, the night we lost Mama.

That night we waited on the fence for Pa too. He'd gone to town to look for someone to help Mama deliver the new baby, the eighth child, but the midwife could not be found. He returned empty-handed and looked mighty worried. He slammed on the brakes and jumped out of the car, then gave an anxious look toward us kids on the fence. He lifted Gracie off the fence and was about to put her down when we heard Mama scream in pain like a wounded wolf. Pa ran into the shack with three-year-old Gracie running after him crying.

"Get back out there Gracie," he yelled. "Dolly, come take care of your sista'. Ya'll don't belong in here now."

Dolly ran into the house to snatch Gracie and carried her back out by the rest of us.

"Hush now, little one. Pa said we need to wait until Mama has the baby. Then we can go in." She cuddled the toddler and smoothed her hair until Gracie stopped crying.

"Mama's in trouble," Dolly whispered to Guy and me out of earshot of the rest. "I saw her, Guy. The bed was all bloody. Looks like she's dying. Pa's face was all white. He looks scared. He didn't find anyone to help. He doesn't know anything about babies."

"He will tell us when it's all right to come in; he always does," said Guy.

Our attention was drawn to Jesse's cries. He'd fallen off the fence again, for the third time. We laughed at him for making a huge scene, acting like he was hurt. "I broke it! I know I broke it!" he cried. He did all he could to get a laugh. We knew that fake cry. He used it too many times already. Still he tried to convince us he had broken his leg. Then we saw Pa at the door, still as a statue, with a blank look in his eyes. His shirt was covered in blood.

Josie jumped off the fence and ran towards Pa. "Brother or a sister?" she blurted out.

He pushed her aside, as if he hadn't seen nor heard her. Pa's face was ashen, rolled into a scowl. His eyes were red and puffy. I sensed something was very wrong.

"Pa?" Josie looked up at him with sad eyes of a kicked puppy. "What's wrong?"

"What's wrong, Pa?" Dolly asked. "Is Mama okay? What about the baby?"

Pa wouldn't – couldn't – speak. Just motioned woodenly toward the shack and stared past us; then he turned around and went back inside. We knew now wasn't the time for questions, and headed for our bunks. No arguments. We were cold and glad for a warm bed. Plus, we were afraid to ask.

Funny, I thought. Can't hear a baby crying. Probably asleep already. I'll find out if I have a brother or sister in the morning. I drifted off to sleep.

Next morning I rushed to Mama's bed to see the new baby, but all I found were blood-soaked sheets. Couldn't remember hearing a baby cry during the night either, come to think of it. The house had been way too quiet. Now, we couldn't find Mama anywhere and the baby's crib was empty.

I caught sight of Pa through the window. He still wore the bloody shirt and he had not combed his hair. His overalls were dirt-crusted and mud covered his hands. He had the saddest look I'd ever seen. He was heading back from behind the barn with a shovel in hand.

The awful realization hit me hard when I looked from where he'd come. There were two small crosses pushed into mounds of freshly-shoveled dirt. I knew then why we couldn't find Mama – and why I never heard a baby crying. They were both gone. Forever.

C.A. SIMONSON

5 Fence Thinkin'

And here we were again –sitting on the fence
waiting for Pa, but we didn't even know where he was
or why he left. He only told us to wait. It made me
worried – for him and for us kids.

Dolly had fixed a small vegetable stew from the
little food she found. We had just finished our supper
when Pa came home. He entered the shack and
slammed the door. He was already half-drunk by the
looks of him. He pulled a few coins from his pocket
and threw them on the counter by the sink. He dug
through the cupboards, looked in the refrigerator,
then back to the cupboards again.

"Pa, did you bring any milk from town?" Dolly
asked. "I used up all the food we had here."

He gave her an angry stare, then looked at each of
us around the table with a strange look. We could
smell liquor on his breath again.

"I cain't do this anymore," he shouted, a little too
loudly.

"Pa, you're just tired and hungry. Please, sit and
eat."

He shook his head at her. His eyes looked wild.

"Pa, please sit down," Dolly tried to soothe his
anger.

"Cain't eat. Not hungry. Gotta go to town. Ya git
your coats on and git outside."

We didn't listen at first. Thought the drink was
talking again, so we ignored him. Should have known
better.

"Didn't ya hear me?" He grabbed Guy's chair and
yanked it out from under him. Guy fell to the floor,
but jumped up quickly. "I said, git yourselves outside.

Now." He took a swing at Guy, but Guy ducked away. At the same time, Guy caught Dolly's eye. She knew what to do. Guess we all did.

We grabbed our coats and hats on the way out the door, and hoped Pa's rage would be over before Guy got hurt.

"Ah've had enuf," he yelled. He kicked Guy out the door with a boot in his behind. Watched in unbelief as Pa locked the shack, staggered to his truck and weaved it down the road. He spent the money that would feed us and didn't seem to know what else to do. Mama had been the one who took care of us, not Pa. He couldn't hold down a job and couldn't keep the money from dwindling away. So, he did what he always did when he didn't know where else to put us. He hooked the little one atop the fence by her coat and told the rest of us to get on our fence post. We thought it would be just like the other times. He would be back. No matter how long it took, he always came back.

The air got colder as dusk settled in. I tightened the woolen scarf around my neck and braced my back against the wind. My thoughts drifted back to the terrible day we lost Mama. It was cold like this that day too, almost one year ago today.

Pa took to drinking more and more after that awful day. Dolly tried to keep house and care for the little ones. She did her best to cook, clean, and care for the little ones, but Pa never seemed satisfied. He yelled that there wasn't enough, but he never brought much food or supplies either. Instead, he came home with a bottle or two and went into the other room to drink them down. All the money he did earn seemed to end up in that brown bottle. We could count on him being passed out, drunk somewhere.

Tonight, we were glad Dolly managed to throw a stew together for our bellies' sakes. On this cold night, Pa had no reason for us to sit on the fence.

"Don'cha dare move an inch!" he warned.

He left us all to wonder what was going on. Figured he was going to town to do more drinking, but maybe, just maybe – he went to look for someone to come take care of us. Anyone would do. We didn't care if she was young, old, ugly or pretty. We just needed someone who would feed us and care for the little ones.

We waited and waited on the fence that night playing our silly fence games, told stories, laughed, taunted each other with dares, and tried to keep our minds off the cold. As the sun went down, the colder it got as winter threatened an early entrance. Darkness settled in and made our fence-sitting almost scary as the shadows danced off the grass and trees. Cold wind whipped at our faces as drizzle turned into sleet. Hard icy darts stung my face. Everyone wanted to go inside. Why did he lock the shack? Why can't we go back in? We had to get inside where it was warm and safe, but that decision was up to big brother Guy. He was boss when Pa was gone; after all, he was almost fifteen. Tonight we were more than ready to listen.

"Ah'm really gitting cold," little Gracie shivered through chattering teeth.

"Ya shoulda put your warm boots on," Josie scolded. "Look! Ya don't even have your scarf on. You're okay. Ya won't freeze. Pa will be back soon." She tried to convince her, but none of us were really too sure. Jesse started to cough again; his throat sounded raspy.

"We're all gitting too cold, Guy. We can't stay out here all night, even if we huddle together," Dolly said.

"Dolly, let me down, please?" Gracie cried.

Dolly made a quick decision, jumped off her post, and headed towards Gracie. "I told ya to put on your mittens and scarf, Missie. Now look at ya! Colder than an icicle. Dolly removed her scarf and wrapped it around little Gracie's neck. "Come over by me, darlin'." Dolly lifted little Gracie off her post and wrapped her big coat around her baby sister and hugged her tight against her own body.

"Dolly, what are you doing? Pa will have your hide!" Guy shouted through the wind.

"I don't care, Guy. This li'l one is 'bout to freeze, and I will not see it happen. Somebody has to do somethin' or we'll all catch our death out here. Let him whip me if he wants."

Guy jumped off his perch then and took a look around. "You're right, Dolly. We have to do something. He can whip me too. C'mon everybody," he ordered. "Enough is enough. Follow me."

"But ya know what happens to us if we don't wait for Pa, Guy, and I don't want no whippin'!" Josie cried.

"Whippin' or not, we can't stay out here any longer in this sleet and cold," Guy said.

Guy went to the locked shack door and tried to pry it open. It was already frozen shut with ice. "C'mon," he commanded again. "Tonight we'll stay in the barn. Tomorrow, we'll see what's what."

"I want my Mama," wailed Gracie, her tears threatened to freeze as they rolled down her reddened cheeks.

"And my toes are freezin'," whimpered Josie.

"Stop your bawlin'," Guy snarled. "Ya'll be just fine. You'll see."

The fact was – Pa never did come back that night. And we never saw him again.

6 Cold Night - Warm Barn

Guy pulled his too-small jacket over his head to ward off the intrusive sleet. "Hurry up!" he yelled through the howl of the wind. "Let's git to the barn. It should be open."

Guy picked Gracie up in his arms and headed toward the barn. Dolly adjusted her woolen hat over her ears and shielded Josie from the sleet with her coat and followed.

"Race ya," Mikey yelled at Jesse and made a dash for the barn.

Jesse slipped on a patch of ice as he went into another coughing fit and tumbled to the ground. Guy set Gracie down and kicked at the door a couple of times. We boys took the lead from big brother and kicked at the door too. After several moments, it loosened itself from the icy fingers that held it tight and opened wide. The barn full of old, musty hay gave warm invitation to our cold bodies.

"Dolly, you go over there with the li'l girls. Git 'em settled in. Now, now, Gracie, ya stop your whimpering, ya hear? Ya'll be fine. Brothers, ya'll find yoresef a place to plop. We'll git this figgered out in the mornin'. Fer now, we all jes' need some sleep."

Tired, cold, and achy I just wanted to warm up and go to sleep. Climbed to the top of the hay bales where the loose hay lay close to the hay mow. Dug into the hay for warmth and glanced out the window towards the dirt road. Wondered again where Pa could have gone. "Why is he taking so long? Did something happen to him? Why did he leave us? What will we do if Pa doesn't come back?"

I was thankful for my brothers and sisters. We stuck together. Little Gracie and Josie cuddled up close against their older sister. Dolly's arms were wound securely around them, just like Mama would have done. I smiled, but felt an ache in my heart at the same time. Dolly was so much like Mama. I sure missed Mama. Dolly loved and cared for us all, especially her little sisters. Tears rolled down her freckled cheeks as she cried softly. I swallowed the big lump in my throat, brushed away the tears that threatened to come, and searched to see where the other boys settled. Mikey and Jesse found their spots in the corner and were burrowed in for the night like a couple of gophers. Jesse coughed on and off all night, heard him sniffle and sneeze a few times too. Didn't sound good. He had been sickly his first few years with whooping cough and fevers. Seemed to struggle a lot with coughing or breathing. Guy, our strong, brave brother, was at the barnyard window searching the road. Somehow he knew he was in charge whether he liked it or not. He had to find a way out of this mess for all of us. We knew he had the final say and that was okay. We needed him to be in charge. He was smart. He'd figure it all out. He knew everyone was all right now, and we would all have a good night's sleep. I watched him lay back in the hay. Although I noticed a huge furrow in his brow, he dozed off to sleep almost in an instant.

Sighed and yawned, glad for the warm, dry hay. Pushed my body into the hay until I sunk deep, almost burying my body up to my neck. It reminded me of the time Guy dared me to jump from the haymow into the pile of loose hay below. As I thought back, I got shivers all over again. I never could stand down a dare.

"C'mon, scaredy-cat, jump!" Guy taunted.

So, I held my breath, counted a loud "1-2-3" and jumped head long into the hay below. To my surprise, I sank almost to the bottom of the pile, as if it were quicksand. I was being buried alive in hay. The more I struggled, the further I sank.

"Guy! Guy! Help!" I tried to cry out. The hay pushed up my nose and stuck to my mouth. It smelled musty. I started to feel dizzy. "Guy? You there? Can you hear me?"

Guy was alert to the danger and the folly of his ill-swayed idea. Fearful for my fate, he jumped into the hay and began to rake it with his fingers.

"Timmy! Timmy!" He used my given name. "Are ya all right, Buddy? He tried his best to sound light-hearted like nothing was the matter. "Whadja do? Find a hole in the hay or something?"

His voice was muffled by layers of hay — somewhere? Above me? Felt like I was going to pass out. Couldn't breathe.

Guy spotted the top of my head and pulled at the hay until my whitened face was free. I felt him pull at my arms. Almost unconscious, I tried to open my eyes, but felt woozy. Someone was trying to brush hay and dust away from my face.

"Hey bro'," Guy smacked at my cheeks. "Look what you missed!" He gave a nervous laugh. He pulled Pa's rusty old pitchfork, tines up, out of the hay, just inches from where I had landed. There it lay plain as day.

Guy had tried to act like it was all a big joke, like we'd just had the most fun, but I noticed the anxious look in his eye. His eyes betrayed his fear. His face was all white as if he'd seen a ghost. He had been scared out of his wits, and so was I. We both knew I'd had a close call that day and was pretty lucky.

I must have been quite a sight, covered with sweat and dust from dirty hay head to toe. We never told Pa. He would have skinned us alive if he knew I jumped out of the haymow. If he had known Guy encouraged it, he would have gotten a beating too. No. We didn't said a word. Guy had kept his lip zipped, and so did I.

Guess I was lucky in more than one way that day. Maybe someone was watching out for me besides my brother. Who knows? I thought out loud as I snuggled deeper in the warm hay. It was just good now to be inside where the wind wasn't freezing cold.

7 Parting Ways

Woke up with a start as it felt like something ran across my face. My nose was just inches above the straw. I clawed and pulled my way out of the hay hole my body sunk into. My clothes were drenched in sweat from the all-too-real dream. I peered out the haymow window, and saw the golden sun as it started to peek over the frozen horizon. Everything was frost-covered and cold. It was almost morning. Now what?

Found Guy out back of the barn doing the same job I came to do. "'Spose Pa is in the shack, sleeping it off?" I asked my big brother.

"Nope. Ah already took a look around. Shack's still locked and dark. Guess Pa decided not to come back."

I could tell by Guy's frown that he was more worried than he let on. He also had that look that he'd made some decisions. He seemed older today – more determined, more in charge – more...

"C'mon," he broke my muse.

"The li'l ones are hungry," Dolly said as we walked back into the barn. She finger-brushed the hay out of the girls' hair. "They're whinin' already."

"What ya gonna feed 'em, Dolly?"

"Well, if we can git back in the shack, we could maybe find some left-over stew. Or at least some bread and lard."

"Already thought of that. C'mon y'all. Wake up! Let's go! Ah broke a winder and crawled in. Don't know why Ah didn't think of that last night. Anyways, we can patch it up with a sheet or somethin' later. Don' matter none now. Right now, we jes' need some

35

food in our bellies. Let's git inside." Guy headed towards the shack. Jesse and Mikey followed, rubbing the sleep from their eyes.

Sounded good to me too. We crawled through the broken window into the back room and hurried to the kitchen in hopes of some left-overs of cold stew. No luck – Pa must have dumped it in the garbage. A couple pieces of hard bread were still on the counter. Dolly searched the cupboards for any scraps, but they were empty. Pa hadn't brought home any food this past week. He drank it all away.

Dolly's eyes clouded over and threatened to fill with tears. "Pa promised he was gonna get supplies and stock these cupboards. He knew we needed food."

"Already checked the cupboards, Dolly. Ain't got nothin'. We can't stay here, at least all of us together. Winter's comin'on fast, an' there ain't no way to heat this dump."

"Where's Pa? Why hasn't he come back? Do ya think somethin' happened to him, Guy? Why would he leave us here like this – alone with nothin'? What's wrong with him?"

Dolly looked like she was going to cry, but I knew she wouldn't, at least not in front of the little girls. She had to be brave for them, and she knew it. She dabbed her eyes, and raised her eyebrows at the one in charge as he motioned toward her and me.

"We got some talkin' ta do," Guy whispered to her and me, his voice somber. It was kind of scary. A little shiver ran up my spine. I still wondered what happened to Pa.

Dolly put Mikey, the twins, and Gracie at the table and divided the hard bread crumbs between them. Then she joined Guy and me in the corner.

Guy spoke soft and low so the other kids couldn't hear. "Ah did me some hard thinkin' last night. It jes' don't look like Pa's comin' back this time. If he were, he woulda' bin here already. So this is the only thing Ah could figger. Ya'll ready to hear my plan?"

Dolly's big blue eyes were sad and moist with tears, like she already knew what Guy would say. She too, seemed to grow up even more overnight. Dolly was intuitive beyond her years. She nodded at Guy and gave him a look that said go ahead.

I shrugged my shoulders. Couldn't guess in the least what Guy would have to say. "Guess we're ready, Guy. What's your plan? What can we do?"

"Wahl...." He began and pulled at his stubby chin where a few whiskers threatened to pop through, "...this is how Ah sees it. Can't say as Ah's like it, but there's just no other way to do things." He paused for effect and looked us straight in the eyes.

I could tell he was hedging. "C'mon already," I prodded. "What's your plan?"

He shot me a shut-up-and-be-quiet look, and began.

"Okay. This is it. Ya'll see that there's no food or nothin' here for us to eat. There's no heat, and it'll be gittin' colder fast. Now, the way Ah sees it, Dolly and Ah could go out and git ourselves some work, but then, who would takes care of the li'l ones? And what about school for you boys? Mama's not here to teach us anymore. So here's what Ah've been thinkin'. We should all split up, and go to different people's houses – see who'll take us, and who won't. If nobody wants us, then we'll just keep movin' on til' somebody takes us in," Guy stated without emotion. Had it all figured out.

So that's how it was. Just a matter of fact. What else could he have said? What was I expecting him to say? That we'd go find Pa? That we'd just make do in the shack by ourselves all winter? I was dumbfounded. Gave him a blank stare as he continued.

"Like Ah said, thought about it all night long – doin' some real heavy thinkin' and there ain't no other way. Let's tell the others."

We went over to the table where the others sat, and Guy took charge like a big brother should. All eyes were on him.

"Dolly, you and Josie and baby Gracie, ya'll go over to the preacher's. Tell him what's happened. Tell him Pa left us and never came back. He'll understand. He knows Pa. The preacher's a good man. He'll know what to do. And just maybe he'll know some good family you and the li'l ones can stay with until we find Pa, or 'til he gits back.

Josie and Gracie sat there wide-eyed as big tears formed. Their little lips quivered and their bodies shook as they looked at their big sister for support. Dolly avoided their fearful eyes and stared at the floor.

"Mikey, you and Jesse can maybe go over to the Johnson's. Their girls are 'bout your ages – maybe they will let you stay there a spell. Ah'll go with ya and ask 'em myself. Frankie..." Guy looked me right in the eye. I braced myself for what was to come.

"Frankie, yore old enough to do some work. Old man Wheeler up the road might need help with his harvestin' or his sheep, or plantin' crops come next spring. Why don't ya go ask him if he needs a helpin' hand? He might even let you stay there. Anyway, that's the best Ah kin think of for now," Guy stated.

What? I couldn't believe my ears. I was too shocked and amazed to react right away. Each of us had glazed-over eyes our mouths hung open in disbelief as we stared at our big brother. Could he mean it? Would he make us? After a couple minutes of silence, Dolly spoke.

"And you? What about you Guy?" she spoke in a whisper choked with tears. "Where will you go?"

"Wahl..." Guy looked out the window, as if searching for an answer to appear, then scratched at his chin again.

"...rightly don't know jes' yet. Might go lookin' for Pa in town; ask around, see if anyone has seen or heard from him. If he's not there then Ah'll think about goin' to the next town, and maybe the next. If I find him, we'll come back and find ya'll. Don' ya'll worry about me. Ah can take care of myself."

"Please don't leave us, Guy," Josie wailed. "We need ya!"

Little Gracie was crying too. Jesse and Mikey just sat there with a blank stare. It was now Dolly's turn to take charge.

"Guy's right, ya know. It's the only way for us all to survive. We have no other family. Mama's dead. Pa's gone. We don't have no money. We don't have no food. There ain't no heat. We'll get sick and die if we stay here. It's easier for folks to put up with a few kids instead of all of us at once. It's the only way. It's all we can do... the only way," Dolly repeated, her voice trailing, getting softer and softer until it faded to nothing. She couldn't look any one of us in the eye. I saw those big blue eyes of hers swell up with hot tears. She fought them away, wiping at her eyes with her ragged sweater sleeve. She really did look like Mama now. Mama always had the same look when she was sad.

So it was decided, and off we headed – each in different directions. It's a day I'll never forget – cold and crisp, after the stinging sleet from the night before. We all seemed to know in our hearts that we would never see Pa again – and maybe not each other either. Guy took Mikey and Jesse and began to walk down the road to the Johnson's who lived on the corner. Dolly and the girls went east towards town and the preacher's house.

I didn't like to think that I'd never see my brothers and sisters again. And I sure didn't like the hard knot in the pit of my stomach. Made me feel kind of sick. But, at the same time, I was kind of excited. Couldn't let myself get sad now. I was ready to search for what life was all about.

This was going to be some adventure –and no one to tell me what to do! I was on my own and I had a farmer to visit, and a job to get!

8 New Home New Job

So my journey began. I was on my way to search for new beginnings in life.

Before I headed for the farmer's, decided to head to the fort in the woods. Hoped there was some crackers or jerky down there from summer. Although the sun shone bright on the frost-covered ground, the air was brisk for an October morning. The sight that met me made my heart sink. What happened to our fort? It looked a whole lot different than the way we'd left it last summer. Guess I'd forgotten what rain and wet fallen leaves could do to a dirt hole. It was more like a mud slough. The sides were crumbled in; water sat in a cold glaze of ice. The sticks we attempted to prop up for the roof had long since fallen in. So much for crackers and jerky— and so much for plan one. I sure wasn't going to try to camp out in that mud hole.

Oh well, guess it won't hurt to talk to Farmer Wheeler. The Wheeler's, an older couple, lived a few miles down the road from our place. We didn't pay them much mind; he and his missus kept to themselves. It was early afternoon by the time I reached the farm.

I spotted an old man in bib overalls leaning over the cow tank, just south of the huge red barn. He was thin and had a bushy gray beard. It looked like he was busy dunking something up and down in the cow tank. As I got closer, a chill ran up my back. Did he really have that thing by the throat? The farmer had not seen me walk up the drive. Engrossed in his gruesome task, he gave me a scowl as I neared the tank, then went back to his business as if I weren't there. He released his package into the water. I peered into the tank and watched as the furry 'something' struggled in the water. I saw a pile of furry 'somethings' at the bottom of the tank.

"Whatcha' doin'?" I stared wide-eyed into the tank.

"Dern cat," he muttered, "woulda had us overrun with them squawlin' kits."

Without another word, he turned and walked towards the barn without paying me any more attention than he gave the kittens.

I strained my eyes to look beneath the murky water. I didn't want to believe what my brain said was true. But sure enough, there they were, just as he said: a whole litter of soaked dead kittens at the bottom of the cow tank.

I ran to catch up with the farmer already in the barn by a large mare. Her stomach looked big.

"Ya still here?" he stared me in the eye as he stroked the horse's mane. I stared back and watched him whisper something into the horse's ear.

"Yeah, I mean, y-y-yes, sir," I stammered and looked at the floor. I didn't know what to say. How can I ask if I can live with him? I was scared to ask. What if he says no? Does he toss all the throw-aways into the cow tank? I sucked in my gut and took a deep breath.

"Well, whaddya want, kid?"

"I come to ask if you need help?" My voice felt small.

"From who?" he scowled at me again.

"From anyone..." I hedged and shrugged my shoulders. Took another deep breath and began again.

"From, uh, well, from me," I emphasized a little louder.

"You!?" He let out a loud guffaw. "You're nuthin' but a li'l kid."

"But I'm strong," I argued. "And I can work real hard! Besides, I won't take up much room."

He took a long, hard look at me. "Ya by yourself?"

"Yes sir."

"Where's your Ma?"

"Dead."

"Where's your Pa?"

"Gone."

"No brothers or sisters?"

"No sir. Just me," I lied. "Please, mister. Will you let me work for you? There must be something I can do." I pleaded. I tried to wrinkle my face to look sad. He looked at me real strange, took off his straw hat and scratched his head, then pulled at his bushy beard. Maybe he was giving it some thought.

"Hmmm. Ya live around here?" He belched.

"No," I lied again. He should know me; we're neighbors down the road, I wanted to say, the family with all the kids; but my words wouldn't come out. I was too scared to look him in the face so I stared at the ground. Felt his eyes on me, as if to check me out. The farmer didn't say anything for a long time. Couldn't stand the silence anymore so I blurted out a little too loudly, "I was hopin' to live with you."

Mr. Wheeler stepped back in surprise. He took my arm and felt of my muscles and then tilted my head back to look me straight in the eye real suspicious-like. I felt weird, like he was pricing a new calf from market.

"I'll earn my keep."

Mr. Wheeler didn't speak.

"I'll do anything you ask. I can work real hard."

He pulled at his beard some more and squinted his eyes.

"Hmmm..."he muttered again under his breath, "your freckles aren't even dried on yet."

"I'm a hard worker. Really, I am."

Where's your things?"

"Don't have any."

"Ya don't say. Just a poor urchin without a home, huh?"

I wasn't real sure what he meant by that, but I nodded.

"Well, gotta talk to the missus. But for now, guess ya can shack up here in the barn. Now, go git the broom," he pointed to the corner, "and start sweepin' out all these here horse apples." He gave my butch haircut a rub and walked toward the house.

I wasn't sure what horse apples were, but I headed toward the broom with a big grin on my face. My heart leapt! I'd just landed my first job and found a new home!

9 Wheeler's Barn

Mr. Wheeler returned later with some bread, cheese and milk, and a small woolen blanket.

"Guess ya'll be okay out here tonight, kid," he said. "Nowhere to put ya in the house, mainly because I ain't spoke to the missus yet." He put the food on the ledge of the wooden stall, dropped the blanket, then turned and walked out the door again.

Guessed the farmer was a man of few words. Well, that was okay. Didn't have any more to talk about anyway. I had a place to sleep and food for my belly. Slept in a barn before, I could do it again. Found a clean stall, bunched some straw into a heap, and thanked myself for sweeping up the horse apples. Grabbed one of the horse blankets laying over the edge of the stall and laid it over the straw. Comfortable enough, but nothing like warm hay to snuggle into. I shivered and curled into a tight ball with the small woolen blanket wrapped around me.

I heard the soft snorts of a few horses around me; the large mare seemed uneasy. Heard something rustle in the rafters above me; made me suspect mice or bats? I curled up tighter and shivered again. Closed my eyes and tried to go to sleep when all of a sudden, I heard a chilling scream in the distance that sounded like a frightened baby's cry. Goose-pimples popped out all over my body and a shiver ran up my back. Was there an animal out there who wanted to be in the barn too? Would he sneak in the barn in the middle of the night? Would be better if there was a light on, but didn't want to turn on the overhead lights and alert the farmer. Searched for a flashlight, and found a few rows of shelves along the wall. Most were empty, but there were a few cans of paint, turpentine, a box of matches, some stuff that looked like poison and some other strange jars. Some strange-looking gadgets hung by hooks on the wall. Among them was an old rusty lantern. A lantern may even give off some heat. I was proud of myself. No animal was going to surprise me tonight. Filled the lantern with some turpentine, lit it and set it close by my makeshift bed. Found it didn't offer much more warmth, but at least it would let me know if any critters tried to get in.

Relieved, I felt tired. It had been a long and weary day. I soon fell fast asleep and dreamt of happier times in the woods.

It was a nice, warm summer day and the sunshine felt so good, so toasty. I wandered down to the old pond. The sun was high in the sky and the air was becoming sweltering hot. I listened, but could not hear any crickets or birds. My body dripped with sweat; felt like I was about to burn up —so hot; couldn't breathe.

The dream made a sudden switch with me under water drowning. I gulped for air, and sputtered water from my mouth and nose. Did I fall in the pond? What was happening? I choked on more water. Tried to figure out where I was. Awake? Asleep? Didn't know. I sat bolt upright as water splashed me in the face.

"Help! Help me!" I heard myself say.

Cold water drenched me again, soaking my head and chest. Rubbed at my eyes, tried to wake up. Couldn't figure out what was going on. Smoke was thick and my throat tightened; couldn't breathe. My eyes stung. Coughed hard. Out of burning eyes I saw Mr. Wheeler with another bucket of water ready to douse me again.

"What in the heck you doing, mister?" I sputtered through another drenching. I coughed again. "Trying to drown me?"

I jumped as Mr. Wheeler's foot stomped on the smoking straw where my head had been. Still wasn't quite sure if I was dreaming or not. My eyes darted from Mr. Wheeler's foot to his face. What had I done?

"The question is what were you doing, kid? Tryin' to burn my barn down?

Mr. Wheeler tossed more water on the smoldering straw where I laid. Smoke filled the barn. Must have kicked the lantern over in my sleep. The more I rubbed my eyes, the more they stung.

"Heard the horses – didn't you? Thought Ah'd better check see what they were bothered about. Good thing. Ya woulda burnt the barn down with yourself and all the horses in it." He stomped out the last of the flames.

I looked in despair at the mess I'd made. My first night here and I almost destroyed everything the farmer owned. I was ashamed and sorry, but couldn't think of the words to say. I shrugged my shoulders and hung my head.

"Sorry," I muttered too soft for Mr. Wheeler to hear for his whole attention was already on the stall where the big mare lay.

She pawed the floor, laid down, got back up, then laid down again and made terrible whinnying noises.

"What's wrong with her?"

"She's ready to have a foal, and we're here to help her if she gets in trouble. See there! He's being born now."

I stood there and gawked at the strange new sight. Soon the colt was born. The little guy sprawled on his legs, and then stood upright with a little whinny. He wobbled some, then lay back down. He was a beauty with his maple brown coat and star-shaped patch of white on his forehead.

"Can I name him?"

Mr. Wheeler was not listening. His mind still busy with the mare. "Git over here kid. I need ya. Now." A huge frown creased his face and his brow was stuck in a wrinkle. "Another colt's comin' and it's stuck."

I neared the horse for a better look. Something just wasn't right. All I could see was curled-up legs –like it was coming out backwards.

"Get the come-along, kid," he shouted.

"The what?"

"Hangin' over there on the rack," he pointed to some of the strange gadgets I'd seen earlier. I looked that direction, but was frozen in place. I shrugged my shoulders and stared at him.

"Has a hook and some ropes on it," he explained in rapid, short breaths, "meant for pullin' things. Now hurry up and git it."

I stared wide-eyed at the mare writhing in pain. The farmer whispered in her ear and stroked her mane.

"Now!" he pointed again to the crude-looking instrument in the corner with a growl on his face. I snapped as if from sleep and ran to grab the metal gadget with ropes and hooks and stuff.

"That's it. Good. Now go hook that rope to the post over yonder."

Mr. Wheeler worked himself into a sweat to get the come-along attached to the unborn colt, but couldn't get a good hold on the back leg.

"C'mere – Ah need your help, kid. Stick your hand in there and grab the leg."

I stood there motionless and stared to where the farmer pointed and back at him with wide eyes and shook my head. "I c-c-can't," I stuttered.

"You have to," he ordered. "My arm is too big, and this mare needs some help deliverin' this foal. Just push your hand in real slow-like 'til ya find the leg and git a good hold on it."

I took a deep breath, closed my eyes and inserted my arm. When I found the leg, I inched it to where Mr. Wheeler could tie it to the come-along. Little by little he cinched the rope, and slowly pulled the colt out. The mare wasn't fighting any more. She lay exhausted and very still. Funny how this foal didn't move like the first one did. Too still, lifeless. I raised my eyebrows to question Mr. Wheeler, but now was not the time. His face was bright red; a big frown furrowed his brow.

"Not good. Not good," he mumbled.

The second colt didn't try to stand up. I tried to nudge it a little with my foot.

"Ain't no use, boy. It's dead. Stillborn." He seemed frustrated and mad. "Nuthin' more to do tonight." He gave the mare one more pat and checked on the live colt now lying beside his mother. "C'mon. Ya earned your keep for tonight." He turned and trotted towards the house.

I stood in the barn and stared after the farmer. He was almost out the barn door."

"Wahl, are ya comin' or not?"

10 Meeting with the Missus

The next morning, I awoke to hear the soft voices of Mr. and Mrs. Wheeler at the kitchen table. They thought I was still asleep beside the cook stove where the farmer told me to curl up on the throw rug beside the dog. The collie was nowhere in sight. Didn't want them to know I was awake, so I lay very still to hear what they were saying.

"What's in your head, Stanley, keepin' that, that whelp here? Are ya gittin' crazy, man? Ya know I don't take much to young'uns. Skinny kid like that can't do no hard work here on the farm. Why, he don't even look strong 'nuf to haul water from the well," she said in a whisper.

"Now, Irma, this young'un has had some hard luck already. No family, no belongings. Seems to me he's an orphan needin' a home. I couldn't leave him out in the cold, now could I? He needed a place to spend the night."

"Wahl, he almost burnt down the whole barn!"

It sounded like she spat. Couldn't see her, but searched the room with my eyes and didn't move a muscle. Wanted to hear every word. Couldn't tell what time it was, but the sun shone through the window where old red gingham curtains hung. A small table sat in front of the window where they sat and watched a chattering squirrel on the large oak close by. The kitchen was very small with cracked linoleum on the floor and yellow flowered wallpaper on the walls. Cupboards were few. I smelled burnt coffee on the cook stove above me.

"Where'd he come from anyways?" she whispered.

"Don't rightly know. Seemed as if he jest wandered in from nowhere. Let's wait a few days and see what happens? We could find him a few chores."

I caught a whiff of another rancid smell I couldn't figure out. Then the missus scooped her food scraps into a bucket in the corner. Yep. That was the awful smell. It was so putrid, it made me cover my nose and mouth. Sat straight up and looked at them. They both got real quiet and stared back at me.

I looked down at myself and grinned. I was quite a sight. Dust and straw mixed with blood from the colt stuck all over my coat, pants and hair. I hadn't bathed in...couldn't remember the last time...and had black smudges all over my face. My hair was disheveled and dirty from the dusty barn.

"Where's your outhouse?" I blurted, jumping to my feet. They both chuckled, and pointed outside.

When I returned, a third bowl had been set on the table.

"What ya be called, boy?" Mrs. Wheeler wanted to know.

"My name is Timothy, but everybody calls me Frankie."

"Frankie, huh?

"Wahl, if yore gonna stay with us, ya gotta follow the rules, ya hear?"

I stared at her and pumped my head up and down.

"Now sit. Eat." She poured some sticky-looking grits in the bowl. Her voice was high-pitched and squeaky. She was scary. Her hair was different shades of gray with patches of white here and there. It was pulled straight back into a bun so tight, it made her eyes squint, especially when she looked at me over her wire-rimmed glasses. Or maybe that was just the way her eyes slanted against her fatty red cheeks. Her high-collared dress seemed to scrunch up her whole face.

"What ya starin' at, boy?"

"Nothin'," I lied. I looked down at my bowl of grits and attempted to take a bite.

"Now we ain't rich folks, and we don't got much more than this here farm," she continued. "We really don't have much room or need for any kids."

"But I won't take up much...." I started.

"Don't interrupt!" she said loudly. "Ya only speak when you're spoken to. That's the first rule!"

She said lots more stuff, but I wasn't listening. Her shrill voice reminded me of a sound I'd heard once before; just couldn't wrap my mind around it. Was it the water pump, or that crazy, wild pig Pa had once? It hurt my ears.

"Ya payin' attention, boy?" her voice raised a notch with each word and made me jump back into focus.

"Yes ma'm. Sorry."

She kept squawkin' on and on. Learned she liked to talk. Probably why Mr. Wheeler didn't have much to say. My mind started to wander again in order to drown out her voice. As I scooped grits into my mouth I vaguely heard the word 'food' attached to rule fifteen. Thought I'd better pay a bit better attention.

"...an' ya'll eat anythin'," she emphasized, "anything that's put before ya with no complainin', ya hear? An' ya won't be beggin' for nothin' extra. Ever." she screeched. She let out a little cackle. "'Member Stanley, when that neighbor kid kept comin' over an' beggin' food?" She threw her head back and cackled again. "Wahl, I taught him a lesson, I did, and he never came back again!"

That caught my attention. I stopped chewing and looked straight at her. "What did you a do?" I whispered.

Chuckling, she put her finger in my face. "Wahl, boy, I gave him some of those hot kinda peppers, ya know, those 'halo-peenie' kind? Told him they were sweet like candy and to take a big huge bite, and he did too, didn't he, Stanley?" she crowed. "Funniest thing I ever did see. Went runnin' home to his mama tight as his li'l fanny would carry him screamin' all the way! Never did see him 'round here again beggin' for food. Anyways, as I was sayin', ya'll make sure ya wash your dish when you're done eatin' your grub, and ya'll hang up your coat proper-like on the hook over there. Just 'cuz we're poor don't mean we're sloppy. We're proper folk and we live like it, ya hear, boy?

"I don't think you're..."

"Hush! Ah ain't done yet," she cut me off. "And ya better not be hopin' to git any earnin's 'cuz we ain't got no pay to pay ya with. Ain't that right, Stanley? "

It looked like Mr. Wheeler nodded his head, but did he really agree with everything she said, or was he just trying to ignore her ranting?

"So," she continued her words without end, "keep to yore self and don't bother us none, an' we'll all be just' fine."

"Oh yeah, and after last night, we can't trust ya to sleep in the barn. So, tonight Ah'll fix a place for ya inside."

I wondered about all these rules. Oh well, at least it was a place to eat and sleep. After all, how bad could it be?

"Now eat your grits. They're gitting cold! Stanley, go git some bath water for this filthy kid."

Those grits were the worst non-tasty paste I ever did taste, but I was so hungry, I ate the whole bowl right down. Mrs. Wheeler must have thought I liked them, and gave me some more. Mr. Wheeler brought in a huge washtub and sat it in front of the cook stove. It didn't dawn on me that was for the bath. Water was being heated on the cook stove. She took a pitcher and emptied it into the washtub, one after another, until it was full.

I forced the last bowl of grits down, and thanked the missus. She had a weird gleam in her eye, and I was horrified when I heard her next words.

"Okay, kid. Strip. Time to git ya cleaned up. Yore a mess."

11 Hired Hand

Herb, the hired hand, was already in barn tending the horses. The mess had been swept and cleaned. "What in the world happened out here, Mac? Have some trouble last night?"

Mr. Wheeler glanced at him out of the corner of his eye and nodded, and walked toward the tractor. I followed close behind.

"Figured so." Herb said as he joined him, "already buried the foal and swept up the burnt straw." Herb was a tall, lanky man with bib overalls and cowboy boots. He cocked his head and looked at me with a crooked smile that revealed a few vacant teeth.

"Whatcha got here, Mac? Pick up a stray?"

"Wandered in here yesterday. Yessir. Orphan."

"You keeping him?"

"Looks that way for now. No family. No one to miss him."

"Got yourself some help, then," Herb whistled through the space in his mouth and chuckled. "Ready for that baling job today?"

"Yep. Gotta git it done before the snow flies."

"C'mon, kid – get a move on then! We're gonna teach you how to bale hay," Herb said, still chuckling to himself.

I'd never baled hay before, so didn't know what to expect when Mr. Wheeler handed me a strange thing that looked like a steel claw.

"You're gonna put that claw on just like this, kid – see here? Make sure ya hold on tight."

I did what he did, but it kept falling off my hand. Herb tied the claw to my small wrist so it wouldn't slide off. "There ya go," Herb nodded, proud of his job.

Herb and I hopped on the wagon; Mr. Wheeler got on the tractor. I balanced myself against the wagon's side as we rumbled over the bumpy road toward the field. Mr. Wheeler didn't have much land, but enough to make feed for his horses, and grass for the sheep to graze.

I was fascinated as each hay bale was formed. The baler swooped up the hay, ran it through the loud machine, and it came out the chute in a neat packaged hay bale wrapped like a Christmas present. Soon bales were popping out at a regular rate. Herb grabbed them from the chute with his claw and flung them toward me. I tried to push them toward the back of the wagon. Had some trouble; they weighed almost as much as me.

Around noon when the sun was high in the sky, we took a break for lunch, then went back to work. Evidently, Herb thought I needed to help a little more.

"Hey kid!" Herb yelled. "Tell you what. Why don't you try to grab one of those bales? It's easy. Just plant your feet solid, like this," he put his feet a little ways apart, "then grab the bale with your claw when it pops out of the chute."

I nodded, planted my feet, tightened my grip on the claw, and got ready for the next bale to pop out. You can do this, Frankie, I told myself. Truth was, I was scared.

The next bale popped out and with all the strength of my 78 pounds, I sunk the steel-like fingers deep into the bale. Tried to slide it towards Herb, but it wouldn't move. Felt like the bale was pulling me. Couldn't get the hook out. The tractor started to go downhill and the bale slid toward the edge of the wagon instead of to the back where it belonged.

"Let go, kid," yelled Herb. But I didn't know how. The claw, tied tight to my wrist, was embedded firmly in the bale and wouldn't come loose. Suddenly, the tractor hit a bump, and the bale toppled over the side of the wagon. My small body toppled with it. The bale landed only a few feet in front of the right back wagon wheel.

I heard Herb yell at Mr. Wheeler to stop the tractor, but he didn't hear. The tractor kept coming closer. My fingers were pinched tight into the bale by the claw. I yanked with my arm and pushed with my feet, but couldn't free myself. Didn't have enough strength. Yanked harder. Wouldn't budge. The tractor jerked a bit as the wheel hit the bale. I looked for a way to flop out of the way, but there was nowhere to roll. The wheel was just inches from my head as it started to roll over the bale. I was about to die! I closed my eyes and waited. Then the wagon jolted abruptly to a stop.

Frankie!" Herb jumped off the wagon and rushed toward me. Mr. Wheeler looked back to see what had happened. All he could see was a pair of small legs underneath the bale.

"Oh no, no, no! Frankie! No! Lord have mercy," Mr. Wheeler ran as fast as his 70-year-old legs would carry him.

Herb was already kneeling by my side. His eyes were moist like he could cry and his face was white. "You okay little buddy? Ya break anything?" He squeezed my legs to feel if they were in one piece.

I was dazed. Couldn't speak. Didn't seem real.

"What happened Herb? What happened?" Mr. Wheeler's hands were shaking. He looked scared.

Both Herb and the farmer checked the wheel and dislodged the bale caught in the axle. "Well, won't you lookie here. Looks like this old bale here protected you, Frankie," laughed the farm-hand in a high-pitched, nervous voice.

"It looks like the bale caused the axle to seize up and stopped the wheel just before it reached you, Frankie. It woulda crushed your head for sure. Look. The wheel actually rose in the air over and above your body."

Herb removed his straw hat and scratched his head, shaking it back and forth. He wiped the sweat from his forehead. "You sure you're okay?"

I nodded, but I was still too scared to speak. Herb's hand shook hard as he wedged the claw from the bale, then untied it from my wrist. "Can you get up? He shook his head again as he helped me up.

I stood up slow, but my legs hurt. I was dazed, twisted and bruised, but alive.

"Somebody musta' been watchin' out for you, boy," the farmer commented. "Ain't no way you should be alive." He shook his head as he helped me up. "Just a plain miracle, that's all," his voice small and quiet, "a miracle. C'mon up here with me, kid." His voice waivered.

He put his arm around my shoulder and walked me to the seat of the tractor. He brushed at the water in his eyes with the back of his hand. "No more pitchin' bales for you for the rest of the day. You're ridin' with me."

Grateful, I climbed up on to the side of the tractor beside the old man and sat on the fender. Not another word was spoken the rest of the afternoon.

12 Rules

It was way past dark by the time we got back to the house. I was so tired, just wanted to go to bed. Mrs. Wheeler set some kind of soupy-looking brown stuff in a bowl before me.

"Here's your grub, kid," the missus said, "an' ya better eat all of it."

It didn't look good. It didn't smell good either. In fact, the smell made me sick to my stomach. My body ached and my eyes wouldn't stay open. I nodded off a few times, despite the disgusted looks sent my way from Mrs. Wheeler. Couldn't eat. Too tired.

"Can I go to bed?"

"Yore not done with your suppa'," she hissed.

"But I'm not hungry. I just want to go to bed. Please? I can't eat."

"Let him go now, Irma," Mr. Wheeler said softly, "he's had a hard day."

She raised her voice. "Hard day? Hard day? I had a hard day. Poo! He needs to folla the rules!"

"Another day, Irma. Not now. Let him go to bed."

"Poo!" she spat. "Very well. C'mon, then," she motioned with her hand.

Tried to make my mouth smile and nod a thank you at Mr. Wheeler. Followed her to a little closet-like room under the stairs. She pulled up a trap door and handed me a flashlight. "Down there," she pointed into the darkness. "Pull the string to the light when you get down."

I climbed down the wooden steps into the darkness. I found the string to the light and pulled it. The tiny room filled with dim light. It was damp and cool; appeared to be a root cellar. A couple bushel baskets full of apples sat on the dirt floor. The fresh fruity aroma smelled wonderful. An old green army cot fit snug against one wall. Pulled the light off and crawled under the scratchy woolen covers.

I awoke the next morning to a blend of pine wood burning in the cook stove and the rich cinnamon-sugary-apple smell of apple fritters. Pulled on the light and gazed at my new quarters. Jars and jars of canned vegetables lined the dirt shelves; more sacks of potatoes and squash lined the floor. Just opposite the cot seemed to be a curious, small hole on the upper shelf in the dirt wall. It looked big enough to crawl into; I'd have to explore that sometime. Right now, my stomach growled for something to eat. Hadn't eaten a real meal for a few days, and yesterday's grits and sandwich hadn't filled up my stomach much.

Followed the wonderful aroma up the stairs, anxious to sink my teeth into a warm fritter. Instead, the horrible bowl of cold, watery-brown soup was at my place on the table. I thought Mrs. Wheeler must have forgotten to empty it and wash out my bowl.

"Ya set yourself down now, boy, an' eat your breakfast."

"Can I have a fritter?" I pointed towards the hot stove. The fresh, steaming hot, cinnamon scent sent a rich aroma across the kitchen. Made my mouth water and my stomach growl.

"No, siree, sir. Them is for the mister an' me, not you. Ya didn't finish your supper last night. 'Member the rules? Ya gotta eat what's put before ya. Once ya do, then ya can have something else, not before. So eat your grub."

I stared at the bowl before me. It was the worst thing I ever did see in a bowl. Looked like somebody vomited. I dipped the tip of my spoon in the 'soup', and in slow motion touched the cold stuff to my tongue. Ugh! Just couldn't do it. It was plain awful.

"I can't do it, Mrs. Wheeler. Please, I can't. Please, can't I just have a fritter instead? I promise to finish all my food next time."

"No!" she shrieked. "Rules be rules. If ya won't eat yore grub, then ya gets nothin' 'tall. Be off with ya then. The mister's waitin' for ya in the barn!"

"But I'm hungry." I scrunched up my face and tried to look sad but it didn't work.

"Not hungry enough, Ah reckon," she growled. "Now hurry yore self out the door – he's waitin' on ya."

I hoped she would change her mind and feel sorry for me, and just maybe bring some fritters for morning snack, but she didn't. I brushed the horses and swept out the barn. We worked all morning without any breaks. My stomach ached. I regretted that I didn't grab an apple from the cellar.

Lunchtime finally came. My stomach voiced its void by some loud noises I couldn't control. I hurried to the table only to find the wicked bowl of cold soup still staring me in the face. She didn't even bother to warm it up.

So this was how it was going to be, huh? Well, I can play this game too, I thought. I can be just as stubborn. "Think I'll just go back to the barn and wait on you, Mr. Wheeler. I'm not really hungry." Refused to look the missus in the face. Pushed my chair back, got up and headed towards the door.

"Suit yore self, kid," he mumbled, as he pushed a piece of cheese into his mouth. Makin' that apple pie for supper, Irma?"

She nodded in response, "Yep, plan to can the rest of them apples today too."

No! Not the apples, I thought, horrified. I counted on at least one cold, crisp apple before bed tonight. That may be the only good thing left to eat.

Suppertime rolled around and I was starved. The house smelled of fresh-baked apple pie, crispy fried chicken, and mashed potatoes. I closed my eyes and inhaled a deep breath. Could almost taste it. Felt faint I was so hungry. It had been twenty-four hours with no food and my stomach felt like it touched my backbone! I sat down eager to get my belly full. I was sure Mr. Wheeler would let me eat supper after I worked so hard all day. He must have seen how I'd proved my worth today.

"'Member the rules, boy," she whispered in my ear. Her voice hoarse, her breath like a sewer, that's all she said as she set the horrible brown stuff before me for the fourth time.

I pleaded with my eyes at Mr. Wheeler, but he refused to look at me. My stomach tumbled something awful as I looked and smelled this rubbish that belonged in the scrap pail.

"Can you at least warm it up?"

"No siree. You missed yore chance for hot soup last night."

I forced myself to put a full spoonful in my mouth and swallowed. Almost gagged, but couldn't let them know how disgusting it was. Tasted like rotten fish. Pretend it's pudding, I told myself.

"If it comes back up, ya eat it again, ya hear?" her beady eyes focused at me.

Refused to look at her. Closed my eyes, took a deep breath and downed another spoonful. Tried to plug my nose with one hand and eat with the other. Another spoonful, then another. Though it threatened to come back up, I kept forcing it down, and refused to look at either of them. Shoved the last spoonful of the awful stuff in my mouth, and held my stomach. I was full, but my stomach felt hard as a rock. It hurt; felt like I was going to lose it. Washed down the foul taste with the glass of warm milk and pushed my chair back.

"Going to bed."

I headed toward the cellar, holding my stomach with one hand, my head with the other.

On the way down the cellar steps, I heard the missus whisper with a wicked giggle, "See? I told ya he'd eat it if he got hungry enough."

The old woman sure didn't help me like her much. I crawled under the covers without turning on the light or bothering to change clothes. The knot in my stomach gave another twist and made me double into a ball. I groaned into my pillow, pulled the scratchy woolen blanket over my head, and turned toward the wall. I swiped a stubborn tear that dripped down my face. I missed my brothers and sisters; I missed my mama. I so longed for her hug; it had been so long since I felt a hug.

A little later, I heard the trap door open and someone sneak down the stairs in the dark. I laid in silence, though my gut screamed in pain. The dim light came on as someone pulled the string. I peeked from under the blanket to see Mr. Wheeler watching me. Concern wrinkled his face. He sat down on the floor beside the cot and put his hand on my shoulder.

"Sorry about the missus, son," he began. "Here. Drink this. It will help your bellyache."

I took the glass without question and drank it down. It helped get the awful taste out of my mouth.

"It's been a rough week, Frankie, and I'm sorry ya had to go through all this stuff. Almost thought I was gonna lose you a couple times. The missus can be a might gruff now and then," he apologized. "Ya just gotta take her rules with a grain of salt. She ain't had much luck with young 'uns since we lost our two boys. It's hard for her to get close to anybody, 'specially a kid. She's kinda bitter, but she means well, son." He patted my shoulder again.

Whatever he gave me to drink didn't help my stomach; it made it worse. Made me feel like I would throw up.

"Mr. Wheeler..."

"Call me Mac, son."

"... a bucket – quick!"

"There, there. Feel better now?"

I nodded, but still felt sick to my stomach. Mr. Wheeler sat and talked with me a long time that night. He told me about the two sons he once had – and lost. Though a man of few words, I found when he did speak it was worth the listen and I best pay attention.

13 Two Sons Lost

"Me and the missus married way too young," Mac
said. He rubbed my belly as I laid my head on the cot.
He shook his head, and then looked straight in my
eyes, real serious-like. "Frankie, ya make sure ya get
the right woman someday. Marriage is for life and it
can be long and hard, ya hear?"

I nodded; he continued. "Wahl, we got married
anyways. I was only 18; Irma was 16. We had nuthin'
but ourselves, so we decided to find some land out
west and start a family."

Mac told me they discovered a beautiful river in hill
country in the Midwest, decided to squat on the land,
and call it home. The first summer they lived in a
make-shift tent. When the snow began to fall, Mac
built a make-shift lean-to to provide some shelter. The
light of their lantern and a fire pit gave them light
and warmth. The first winter almost became their
last as the winter storms raged and snow
deepened.Their first baby boy was born that cold
winter.

"We were so happy to have a son," Mac said, "but it
was the coldest winter ever. It got way below zero –
way too cold for a baby. He got a bad cold when he
was a few months old, and then pneumonia and croup
on top of it. He was so sick, and the doctors were in
town more than thirty miles away. We couldn't travel
in the blowin' snow; the doctor couldn't come to us,
and we couldn't git to him. There was nuthin' we
could do except try to keep the baby warm and fed.
The little guy coughed so hard his whole body shook,"
Mac reminisced softly.

Mac was quiet for many moments. I dared not ask questions and break his silence, so I waited.

Mac let out a huge sigh and began again. "He couldn't breathe, and finally he refused to eat. Irma tried her best to nurse the baby. She held him close to her for warmth, but the baby shook with cold and fever. He kept coughin' and wheezin'; couldn't get his breath. He stiffened with pain, and then relaxed, only to go through the same thing all over again. After a few days of it, he gave up the fight; his sick little body became limp in his mama's arms. We hoped he had gone to sleep. Irma held the baby close in her arms and leaned up against the cold, damp, dirt wall and fell asleep. I put more blankets around them both and sat down by my wife. We were both so tired, we fell asleep sitting there.

The next morning, I was startled awake by the sound of Irma's scream. The once-limp baby in her arms was now stiff and blue – cold as the icicles that clung to the door. Irma shook with sobs as she washed his little body. She took a sheet and bundled him like a mummy. I had to make a casket to bury my first-born son."

I heard Mr. Wheeler catch a sob before it came out.

"Frankie, it jest wasn't right to bury my little boy, but I had to. I made a crude casket out of his crib, and buried him in the snowbank behind the lean-to. It was a real hard winter, Frankie. It was so cold and the snow so deep, we had to wait until spring when the snow melted and the ground was soft enough to dig a hole to bury him proper-like. We suffered a lot that year. Irma and me, she's had more than her share of grief, but we've stuck together. By the next summer, she was expecting another baby. We hoped we would have another son, but we were also fearful."

"What happened then?" I dared to ask.

"Well, first I built a sturdier sod home for more warmth and protection. We got ready for the new baby and by October, another beautiful baby boy arrived. We were happy again."

Mac paused in his story. "That is one reason why the missus is so cranky, Frankie. It's October and she is reminded of Jimmy's birthday. Of course, he would have been grown by now, but you make her think of him all over again.

Jimmy was a happy little guy – full of energy, curious about every new thing, excited about life, and bubbled with laughter at his new finds. He learned to walk early, and it was all Irma could do to keep up with him. Jimmy picked up everything he found, had to touch it, turn it over in his hands, feel it and smell it. Often, he had to taste it too. His mother caught him lots of times with bugs or pebbles in his mouth. That's what we figgered happened that terrible day just before Jimmy's third birthday.

Irma was busy in the kitchen making a cake; she thought Jimmy was in the other room playing. He usually came when called, but that day he didn't. She looked all over the house for him. It was a warm October day, so she figured he wandered outside. She called and called, but no answer. She ran to the barn all frantic-like, crying. She said she couldn't find Jimmy. I just finished spreading a bag of purple poison pellets along the edges of the barn to get rid of the rats.

I tried to calm her down, and let her know the boy was probably hiding or playing somewhere. We hunted around the barn and the yard, poked under bushes and lifted boxes where he may have hidden. On the way back to the house, Irma thought she saw a little leg under the porch. She screamed and ran toward the house. We found Jimmy curled up in a ball underneath the porch holding his tummy. I thought Irma was going crazy, she shrieked and groaned so much; couldn't stop her." Mac pulled at his beard and thought a moment, "As I think back now – maybe she did go crazy.

Irma probed his tiny mouth with her fingers. Purple foam oozed from his mouth. He didn't move; his eyes were rolled back. His skin was blue.

My heart sunk to the pit of my stomach. I knew right away what happened. I knew what the purple foam meant. It was the deadly poison, but we had to try to save him. I picked Jimmy up and we rushed to town to find a doctor, but it was too late."

Mac got real quiet again – longer this time. I heard him sniffle, then blow his nose hard.

"I'm sorry, Mac," I offered, but it didn't feel like the words were enough.

"We don't talk about it none, Frankie. Never have. But I wanted ya to know. Maybe now ya understand why the missus is like she is – ya know – bitter and all. We couldn't stay there in that place, so we picked up and moved here to Nebraska soon after that. We had each other, and that was going to have to do. Never tried for more kids. Irma didn't want to go through it again. Now, don't ya ever bring it up or ask questions. What's done is done. Understood?"

Mac gave me one last pat on the shoulder. "Hope ya feel better in the mornin'." He said his goodnight and left me in the dark to think.

From that time on, Mac became a guiding force in my life; a man I could look up to and trust. And maybe, just maybe, I became like a son to him – two had been lost, but one found.

I wanted to become the son Mac never had.

14 Deer Hunt

Winter did indeed come early that year and by November four inches of snow already blanketed the ground.

"It's huntin' time, Frankie," Mac announced one day. "Are ya ready to put some wild meat on the table? "You're almost old enough to carry a gun, but not quite yet. We'll work on that next year, but, yore old enough to go in the woods with me," said Mac.

"What kind of wild meat? Squirrel? Rabbit?" Mama used to fix squirrel pie, and Dolly roasted rabbit a few times I remembered.

"I'm talkin' big game," Mac teased as he saw my excitement grow. My eyes got as big as saucers.

"Are we gonna hunt elk? Or bear?"

Mac let out a chuckle. I'd never heard him laugh before. "Nope. Bear don't live in these parts. Elk neither, but I've seen signs of some pretty big buck. The trackin's and the scrapin's tell me so. And you're gonna push that big one right out to me! I'm gonna git ya to drive the woods for me, boy!"

"But I don't know how to drive. How can I push one to you?"

Mac laughed out loud again. "All ya need to do is walk through the woods and make lots of noise." Mac motioned with his arms and legs. "Wave your arms, kick the leaves, sing. I don' care. Jest scare them deer right my way. Ya can do that, can't ya?"

"Sure!" Sounded like fun. I'd never seen Mac so animated. He seemed almost as excited as me.

"We don't even have to wait until Saturday. We'll go tomorrow. No chores."

Very, very early the next morning, way before daybreak, Mac and I packed on layers of clothes and headed to the woods on the edge of his land. It was crisp, cold, and pitch black. Hardly any stars lit the sky. Even the moon was hidden from view. It was hard to see where to put my foot and I stumbled a few times on the snowy path.

"Frankie, wait here by this big tree, and count to a hundred. Then start headin' my way. I'll be at the other end of the woods. Ya won't see me, but just keep comin' in a straight line. Don't forget to make a lot of noise so ya'll scare that big buck towards me."

Being in the woods again was almost like being home. Made me think of the fun days in the woods with Mikey. We hunted squirrels, birds, and rabbits. Heck. We could have lived in the woods.

I sat down under the big oak and looked up through the empty branches. Couldn't see the top, but it had some low limbs with only a few leaves left. It made me think about my brother Mikey just a few years ago. I smiled. Mikey decided to climb to the top of a tree to see how far he could look. I loved my brother, but sometimes he just didn't think. I chuckled to myself. He got up to where the branches swayed under his weight. Then he either got too excited or scared, or maybe it was just his old Mikey curse. His foot slipped off the branch which made him lose his grip on the branch above him. Saw him falling through the branches, then all of a sudden the cords of his hood caught on a twig. The hood of his jacket cinched up tight around his face and left only his nose sticking out. There he dangled from the limb, swinging back and forth. It was the funniest sight. He screamed his head off for someone to help him. It was so funny, I didn't know whether to laugh out loud or be scared and call for help. The more he wiggled and squirmed, the further he inched out of his jacket. He wasn't high enough to hurt or break anything, so I told him to pull his arms out of the sleeves. He did, and down he crashed onto the soft leaves on the ground. Knocked the wind right out of him. Sure did scare him. Me too. He caught his breath and we both started to giggle so hard we couldn't breathe. We didn't dare tell Mama, but it was a good laugh. Made me miss my brother all over again. I sighed deeply and started the count.

The sun began to peek through the darkness and brought the woods to life. Snowbirds started to chirp. I had counted to one hundred. Jumped up and headed toward Mac. Half-way through the woods I banged the trees with a stick and yelled at the deer but did not see any. Mac was at the other end of the field. He had counted on me to push the big buck toward him, and I didn't want to let him down. I saw Mac perched in a tree when the sun glistened off the barrel of his shotgun.

"Git down kid!" Mac whispered somewhere above me.

"Huh?" I squinted my eyes to find him. I was close enough to see the icicles on his beard and mustache.

"Shhh! Lay down flat. Now! There's one comin' right at ya!" He motioned with his hands to lay flat.

Knew better than to ask questions so I flopped on my belly into the snow, but I couldn't see or hear anything. Rolled over to face the sky and raised my head enough to see the biggest buck ever headed straight toward me!

"Stay down kid! Flat!"

I pressed my head and body flat into the snow. Heard the buck give a low whistle and snort. He smelled me, but couldn't see me. My body shook; tried to be still and quiet. In a flash, the huge animal jumped right over top of me, just inches from my face. The buck never saw me. Mac took his one and only shot and dropped the deer dead in its tracks. I jumped up and ran over to where the deer lay. It was the biggest deer I ever saw.

Mac climbed out of his stand. "Count 'em Frankie."

"...nine, ten, eleven, twelve!! This one's got twelve points, Mac!"

"Yore a mighty lucky, kid," Mac exclaimed with a low whistle. "One clip of those hooves, and it woulda sliced ya straight through. But ya' did good. Ya brought him my way, and I'm real proud of ya. Now I'll show ya how to gut him."

15 Winter of '37

Mac taught me a lot that winter – how to drive for deer, dress a deer, and how to care for horses. The most important thing was how to get along with his missus – and that wasn't easy.

The winter of 1937 came on full force. Blinding snow and complete whiteouts made it difficult some days to even find the barn, let alone care for the animals. More than once I forgot to hang up my coat or put my boots against the wall. Next day when I went to put on my coat and boots I couldn't find them.

"Out in the snowbank, mister," the missus informed me. "If ya can't hang 'em up, that's where they'll be."

You would think I would have learned after the first time. Not me. I was never too good with rules, and I had more than my share of "learnin' times" with Irma Wheeler, from wearing a frozen coat to eating off a dirty plate. It was a good thing I liked Mac and he liked me. It made things bearable, and he most often eased my misgivings.

Chores were still expected to be done whether the snow was blowing or not. Animals still had to eat, and it was my job to feed them.

The blizzard that hit in January was a rough one leaving a frozen tundra with some casualties. Mac was lucky not to lose any animals, but we learned later that some farmers did lose cattle or horses to the cold or lack of shelter.

After the brunt of the storm ended, I headed out to feed and care for the horses. The air was cold and crisp. The snow sparkled like millions of diamonds in the early morning light and crunched under my feet as I walked. As I gazed across the fields; it looked like everything was endless white – smooth and flat, like a soft fuzzy blanket covering the land. The snow came up to the bottom of the window sills and made the five steps up to the house disappear.

I stepped off the porch where I thought the steps would be and landed chest-deep in the snowbank. Tried to make some sort of path through the snow, but must have gotten turned around. Although I headed in the direction of the barn, I forgot about the cistern that was between the barn and the house.

All of a sudden my feet disappeared from beneath me as I fell into the deep hole in the ground. Snow tumbled in on top of me, burying me in the fluffy white stuff. I tried to scream, but the snow stifled any sound. Felt choked. Think. Don't panic, I told myself. I pushed away snow around my nose and mouth to create a small air hole. Think, Frankie. How do I get out of here?

I moved my legs up and down to get warmth in my legs and found the snow started to pack underneath my feet, forming a little mound. I stepped on top of the mound and stomped some more. At the same time, I clawed the snow above me with my red, cold, mitten-less fingers. Little by little, I found myself moving higher – a little closer to the top of the hole each time.

I'm not sure how long it took. It seemed like hours of stomping and clawing the snow. At last, found the top of the hole and crawled out, exhausted. It was starting to get dark when I went into the house.

Crusted with snow, I crumpled in a heap onto a kitchen chair. My breath came in short gasps and I shook all over, wet and cold.

"Whatcha bringin' all that snow in here fer, boy?" scolded the missus. "You're late for supper."

16 Springtime and Summer

Winter turned to spring and little by little the mountains of snow melted. Spring brought many brand new babies into the barnyard: chicks, colts and lambs.

Mac was excited about the new-fangled fence he and Herb put up for sheep that liked to wander off. It was guaranteed to keep animals from getting out, he was told.

Mac and the missus were good at keeping me busy. Along my other chores, work never seemed to end. They always found new jobs for me to do.

"Today we're choppin' tails," Mac said. "Got us ten lambs to do today. Their tails are almost ten inches, and if we don't cut their tails when they're young," Mac said, "they will get infected. I need ya to go catch 'em for me."

"Hey, kid," Herb yelled my way. "C'mere; got something to show you. See this here wire? Grab on to it for me, and hold it down so I can crawl over it, will ya?"

I grabbed the wire like I was told. I let out a shriek like a banshee as the jolt knocked me backwards a couple feet to the ground.

Herb laughed so hard he cried. "See you got the fence working fine, Mac," he laughed again. "Mac likes all the new doohickeys. Has to get them all. See this here, Frankie?" he pointed to a yellow tag on the fence. "That's a warning. Don't touch." He laughed again, and wiped his eyes with his kerchief.

I frowned at him and glanced at Mac. He laughed at me too. "That was a good show, Frankie. Now go git me a lamb."

A newborn lamb, barely able to stand found her mom to suckle. She looked so soft and cuddly. I grinned at the playful lambs running around the field, kicking up their legs, and enjoying the spring sunshine. They shouldn't be too hard to catch.

I spotted one of the smaller lambs first, and decided to tackle him. Tried to sneak up on the little guy, but he saw me first. He waited until I was close, then as I dove headfirst to grab him, he dodged sideways out of my grasp. Sprawled face first into the dirt. The lamb bounded at me, like it was a game. Mac and Herb laughed at me –again.

"Don't let that lamb outsmart you, kid! Go get him!"

"He won't get away again!" I yelled back. Round and round the pen the lamb darted in and out between ewes and bucks. Panting and sweating, I finally chased the lamb into a corner. He backed up further and further until he touched the electric wire. It made him jump and freeze in place. I took advantage of the moment and grabbed the little guy by the neck. Tucked the lamb's head under my arm and held his legs under his body. Mac had the clippers ready.

"Hold him tight, Frankie. He'll jerk hard in a minute."

Mac took the little lamb's tail in his hand and held it out straight. With his other hand he took the big clippers; with one swift clip of the curved blades, the tail was lopped off. The lamb let out a wild bleat and squirmed to get away. My insides squirmed too. It made me jump along with the squealing lamb.

"Almost done. Don't let him go yet," said Mac.

Mac swabbed the lamb's bloody stub of a tail with alcohol making him cry and jerk again with pain and fright.

"Okay. Done. Let him go."

He didn't have to tell me twice. Before I could release my hold, the lamb dug his feet into my ribs and took a wild leap from my arms to scamper back to his mother. I breathed a sigh of relief, glad the job was over. It made me hurt to see the lamb hurt.

"Good job, kid!" Herb praised. "Now, go get another! Just nine more left!"

Chopping tails took most of the morning and part of the afternoon. It half wore me out chasing those lambs. Mac sent me to the house to get everyone a drink of water. The sky appeared sort of grey and dark clouds started to form. Almost seemed like dusk, but it was only the middle of the day.

"Where ya bin, boy?" the missus questioned as I walked through the door. "Ya sposed to bin here an hour ago. Chores don' git done by theirselves, now do they? Soon as your done pickin' eggs and feedin' the hens, I need ya to fetch me a chicken so I can start suppa."

I hated those chickens. Those old hens didn't like me to pluck their eggs from under them any more than I liked plucking eggs. Figured it would be easy to pick up a hen off her nest and take it to the missus. Found out they didn't like being handled any more than lambs. I grabbed at a hen and with a loud squawk, she fluttered her wings, escaped my grasp, and flew from her nest. The whole henhouse erupted into a flurry of feathers. Snatched her up in a quick swoop as she bawked and pecked at my hands, struggling to be set free. Then she did a strange thing. She reared back, stared at my eye, then aimed for it. Startled, I jumped and dropped the hen with a thud. She flew out of the henhouse and the chase was on. My energy was well spent after the lambs, but figured I'd best catch that darn hen. I feared the wrath of the missus more than being tired. I darted toward the chicken. At the same time she flew toward my face. Herb saw the chicken attack, picked up an old tin can and with one shot, nailed the chicken in the head and knocked it cold. I nodded at Herb in relief, grabbed the unconscious hen by its neck and presented it like a trophy to Mrs. Wheeler and half-hoped for a bit of praise. Don't know what I was thinking.

"Oh no, sirree. Ya gotta learn to chop heads today too. Bring me the chicken when it's dead – without the head." She smirked and pointed at a tree stump that served as the chopping block.

The hen started to move in my hand. I ran to get the axe from the barn and delivered the hen to the chopping block. The hen revived from unconsciousness, squirmed and squawked, and flapped her wings again in a frantic attempt to escape. I held her body down with my foot, grabbed her head with one hand, and then stretched her neck as far as it would go. One swift blow with the axe and the chicken's head dropped to the ground. My foot slipped as the headless body jerked off the block. Instead of laying there like a dead chicken, it began to flop all around the barnyard running like a chicken with its head...well, you get the picture.

Had to chase the dadblame chicken again – only this time, it was a headless one. No! Not that way! Tried to catch it but wasn't quick enough. My stomach felt sick as I watched the headless chicken topple right into the open cistern. I'm going to pay for this one when the missus finds out.

I knelt on my hands and knees to look into the cistern when I heard the screen door slam. She ran out of the house as fast as her fat legs would carry her.

"Ya crazy twit!" she screamed. Her face was crimson – her eyes bugged out even further under the tightly pulled-back bun on her head. "Ya can't do nothin' right, can ya?"

"You were watching?" Felt every muscle in my body flinch. If I didn't know better, I would have sworn she had smoke coming from her ears.

"Ya betcha. Gotta keep my eye on ya, boy. Now hike yourself down that hole and git that chicken if ya wants any suppa'," she warned.

"But I couldn't help..."

"What do ya mean, ya couldn't help it? If ya woulda done it right...." She shook her finger in my nose and snarled under her breath.

"But how do I get down there?"

"Ya figger it out kid!" Her voice raised a notch with each word. "Jest do it!"

I peered again into the deep hole that did not appear to have a bottom and searched for the headless chicken.

Mac had watched my chicken-chasing antics with amusement from the barn. He looked at the sky with a frown. It was getting dark way too fast and the air even seemed colder. He came over by the cistern.

"You forgot our drinks, son, but you're funny," he teased. "Ah'll give ya that much. Never catch a chicken before? Ya gotta watch those headless ones," he laughed.

"How am I supposed to get down there?" I gave him a pleading look.

He let out a huge sigh. "Oh, I'll help ya. But we gotta hurry. Storm's a-brewin'."

The wind blew harder, tumbleweeds spun in the air. The sky turned blacker by the minute.

As Mac cinched the rope around my waist, I began to wonder if he were on my side. When he said he was going to lower me headfirst into that deep, dark, stinky hole, I was scared. My mind went back to the first day I met him – when he dunked the kittens in this same well. Would he leave me there? I tried my very best, but things just kept going wrong. Why doesn't anyone love me, I thought as I was lowered deeper and deeper into the hole.

"Mac! Hurry! It's gittin' bad. We gotta git to the cellar!" I heard the missus yell somewhere above me.

Although only half-way down, I felt my body yanked upward with swift jerks until Mac could grab my feet and pull me over the side. My belly scraped the cold cement edge as he hoisted me over the edge. Wind whipped at his clothes, then the sky dumped all its buckets at once. Mrs. Wheeler was close to the house and already soaking wet. I looked to the sky and felt my heart stop.

"Mac!" I gasped and pointed skyward. A huge dark funnel was formed just miles from the barn – headed straight for us.

"C'mon, kid. Hurry! It's a mean twister! We gotta git to the cellar! Now! This way!"

Instead of going into the house, Mac headed to the south side and opened the outside door in the ground that led to the cellar under the house. He pushed me down the steps and hurried in behind me.

"Help me, Frankie. The wind – it's too strong." Mac pulled at the cellar door and the wind pulled back with the force of ten giants. "Grab the rope," he nodded toward the underside of the door. It took both of us to pull the door shut with all our strength, but we managed to latch it tight with us safe inside. Winds howled, and things knocked and fell against the door. I was glad it was heavy and covered with metal sheeting. Nothing could break through. It felt safe down here. The missus sat down on my cot, so I decided to look around.

"What's this here hole for, Mac?" I stood tippy-toed to peer into the black opening in the dirt wall above the third shelf.

"Goes around the house."

"Can I look?"

Mac nodded and pulled at his beard. I found the flashlight and hiked my body up onto the shelf then into the hole on my hands and knees. Part way in, the small beam of light revealed what looked like a narrow, long tunnel. Flopped on my belly and flinched where the fresh wound rubbed the dirt against my shirt. I scooted in further and inched like a snake into the blackness ahead of me.

"Mebbe he'll git stuck," her muffled voice muttered on the other side of the thick dirt wall, but I heard her laugh, loud and clear. Old goat.

The light ahead of me caught a glimpse of something sparkly in the far corner. Maybe a treasure hidden in here – a bag of gold? Jewels? What have the Wheeler's hidden in this crawlspace? I loved a mystery, and I was going to find it! A little further in it felt like the walls were getting narrower. The flashlight served as leverage as I pushed it against the dirt floor to ease myself past the tight spot when everything went pitch black. The flashlight went out and my heart skipped twenty beats. I felt sweaty and cold all at the same time. I realized I couldn't turn around in this hole; must back my way out. Would I fit through the narrow spot again? Breaths came quick and fast; felt faint. I banged the flashlight against the dirt wall until it produced a dim glimmer. I could still see something sparkly in the corner. I shined the light in that direction and imagined it was closer. Was my mind playing tricks on me, or were two eyes staring me in the face? A shiver went up my spine. Something was alive in the tunnel and it was coming my way, getting closer. I had to get out.

I squirmed my body backwards, but felt like I couldn't moving fast enough – the eyes watched my every motion. If there were treasure in the hole, something was there to guard it. Need out. Now. Inched backwards, little by little. Got to the tight spot. Couldn't turn around. Pushed the flashlight against the dirt to push, but it didn't help. That was enough to make the flashlight go out again. Panic set in. Going to black out. Breathe, Frankie. You've been in worse spots. Took a deep breath, put my elbows beneath my body and pushed back again. Nothing. I was stuck tight. Trapped.

"Mac! Mac! Get me out!" Felt like I was yelling into an empty hole. Could he hear me?

Finally, I felt big warm hands wrap around my ankles. Mac tried to pull, but couldn't budge me.

"Frankie, put your arms in front of you," he called into the blackness.

A couple of more tugs and I was out of the dreaded hole in the wall and crusted with dirt. I looked at Mac with wide eyes, my whole body shaking.

"Find anything?" Mac grinned at me. "You're white as a sheet underneath all that dirt."

Shook my head. Wasn't sure what I'd seen in there, but made a mental note to block the opening before I hit the sack that night. Maybe they would let me move back into the barn.

A loud clap of thunder boomed; the house shook as if the roof would cave in or the walls crumble. Mrs. Wheeler screamed and fell to the floor. Then, as fast as it began, it stopped; all was quiet. No sounds of rain, wind, or breaking branches. Mac opened the cellar door a tiny crack to peek outside.

"Oh my, oh my, oh my," he retrieved his kerchief and wiped his forehead. He looked at his wife. "You stay here. I need to check on the animals," Mac said.

I ran up the steps behind Mac and saw what he had seen. A big smile broke out across my face. There were dead chickens and thousands of feathers covering the farmyard.

The tornado that spring was like none other Tekamah had ever seen. Many lost property; homes were flattened; livestock killed. We heard a couple days later that old man Jackson was blown away by the twister never to be found again. Someone said he refused to go to shelter because he wanted to watch the storm. Mac was lucky. A few shingles to be replaced; some fences mended; but the house and barn were okay and all animals spared – except for the chickens. The chicken coop was blown to smithereens and the chickens were gone. I was glad. I hated those chickens. Hoped there would be no more chicken-chasing for this boy.

17 The Pact

It had been almost one year since I showed up at the Wheeler's begging for a home. Things seemed to have settled into a routine: my chores, to sweep the barn, brush the horses, feed the chickens and pick eggs and everything else the missus gave me to keep me extra busy. "Earnin' yore keep," as the missus would say. That fall, I worked with Herb and Mac with baling again.

I had my run-ins with the missus more than once, but guess I was learning her rules. Stayed out of her way for the most part; did my chores and kept to myself. Spent a lot of time in the cellar, but it was my choice. It was my sanctuary; my place to think and be alone.

After harvest was past, Mac announced out of the clear blue it was time for me to go to school; said it just wasn't right to keep a boy from learning. Said he spoke to the teacher, and she was ready for me to start. Figured the missus probably talked him into sending me to school; she didn't like me underfoot. She plain didn't like me. Well, I didn't like her either.

Wasn't sure what to expect from school. Mama taught us what little she knew – reading, writing, but I never attended a real school.

The little one-room schoolhouse sat on the north edge of the little town of Tekamah – about a four-mile hike from the Wheeler's. He insisted I walk. A little afraid, I headed for town with an apple for lunch and a wrapped sandwich made of bread, lard, and sugar. I passed a great looking pond on the way to town and made a promise to myself to check it out soon. The pond was the real temptation, because I knew the fish were biting. I was curious to see what real school was all about. Can't quite say what grade I qualified for, but I was ready to learn.

A young woman greeted me at the door. "You must be Frankie," she smiled. She had long blond hair and blue eyes that were the color of the sky. Sort of reminded me of Mama's eyes.

I nodded, embarrassed because I knew my face turned red. I could feel it.

"Frankie Wheeler, right?"

Sure. Okay. I'll go with that. I nodded again. Best to not blab where I really came from I decided. Besides, it was no one's business.

"Mr. Wheeler told me you'd be here today," she smiled again. I liked the way her eyes brightened, and how white her teeth looked behind her pretty smile. Think I'll like her.

"This is the coat room," she pointed to a row of pegs on the wall. "Hang your coat there and put your lunch on the shelf," she said. She led me into the classroom.

"Did you bring your pencils and paper?"

I shot her a frantic look.

She smiled again. "That's okay if you didn't, Frankie. I am sure someone will share with you today. There's an extra seat behind Michael," she pointed to the far corner of the little room. "Go ahead and get yourself settled in." She patted me on the shoulder and then turned her attention toward the class who were busy in their books. "Children, we have a new classmate today. This is Frankie Wheeler. Make him feel welcome."

I looked over the small one-room school house. Most of the light came from the small windows. There were fifteen or twenty desks in straight rows, with one large desk in front for the teacher. Some desks were empty, but those occupied had kids of all ages. It appeared the older ones sat towards the back, the younger ones in front. The floors were wooden, the windows bare. A little wood stove sat at the front of the building to warm the room in the cold winter months.

I walked to the back of the room to find the empty seat behind this Michael kid. I spotted a boy with his nose in a book a couple years younger than me. That must be him.

As I neared his desk, I couldn't believe my eyes! I blinked a couple times just to make sure my eyes weren't playing tricks. Mikey! My brother? Here? Could it really be? I searched the room again but didn't see Jesse, Josie, or Dolly. Mikey looked at me with a big grin from ear to ear. He was the best sight I ever did see.

Mikey turned around when the teacher wasn't looking and whispered, "You're not Frankie Wheeler! You're Frankie Larue, just like I'm Michael Larue."

"Fittin' name as any," I shrugged. "Anyway, no one needs to know we're brothers. It will be our secret, okay? We'll sign a secret pact and seal it with blood!"

Mikey gave me a puzzled look to ask why, but pumped his head up and down. He loved a good adventure, and he loved keeping secrets even more.

Heard the teacher's ruler crack loudly on her desk. Mikey jerked to attention like someone had yanked his chain. "Is there something you want to share with the whole class, Michael?"

"No, Ma'am. Sorry, Ma'am." Mikey responded almost too politely.

Now what's gotten into that boy? He never minded like that at home. I couldn't wait to talk to him at lunch time.

"So what's up with you Mikey?" I blurted when we got outside.

"I'm glad to see you too, Frankie," Mikey grinned. He grabbed my neck to hug me. Frowned and shoved him to hold him back. He laughed and gave me a slap on the back, then grabbed me again.

"Stop it, Mikey," I warned with another frown. "Is Jesse here? I didn't see him."

"Jesse's sick again today. He's been sick a lot since we went to the Johnson's. You should come see him Frankie. It would make him feel better to see you."

"Well, maybe," I hedged. "What about the girls? Have you seen them? Dolly? Josie and Gracie? Do you know?"

"Nope. Haven't seen them since we left the shack. Figure the preacher found them another place to stay. Jesse really misses his twin sister; I guess I miss the girls too."

"Have you heard from Guy?"

"Haven't heard hide nor hair from Guy; he left, just like you...like everyone." His voice sounded sad. "I thought I'd never see anyone again. Thought it would just be Jesse and me from now on." Mikey's face broke into a big grin, "But in you walked, Frankie, and boy, oh boy, I'm so glad to see you!" Mikey walloped me on the back again, and tried to hug me again.

"I said stop it, Mikey," I made a fist and gave him another push backwards. But in my heart, I felt the same way. It sure was good to see my brother —my best bud— again. It seemed he had grown taller in the year we were apart. He was almost as tall as me now.

The Johnson's must feed him good. He seemed different somehow too; but couldn't put my finger on it. Curious.

"Let's make a blood pact, Mikey – a secret promise, like we used to. I'll write it down, and after school we'll make it official. We'll sign it and hide it."

"Okay, brother! It's a deal," Mikey walloped me again.

"Don't call me brother, okay?" I stared him in the eyes with a stern look. "No one should know we're brothers."

"But why, Frankie? You *are* my brother."

"'Cuz I said, that's why. Okay?"

After school, Mikey walked with me as far as the pond. We searched until we found a real sharp rock. I poked my finger until it bled. Then I handed the stone to Mikey. "Now you poke your finger Mikey."

"Why?"

"'Cuz we're blood brothers and nothing's ever going to change that. We're just gonna be secret brothers. Nothing's ever going to separate us again, okay? Let's make a promise to always be there for each other, no matter what. Okay?"

Mikey nodded and poked his finger too. "Okay, Frankie. Secret brothers. Got it. Promise. Now what?"I grabbed his hand and touched our bloody fingers together. "Now we seal our pact." I dug the hand-written pact from my pants pocket and we both imprinted a bright red fingerprint on the paper. "Let's find a place to hide it so only we know where it is. Remember, it's our secret. Did you bring the pencil box?"

Mikey nodded and produced the box. We signed the pact with our names, folded the precious paper as small as it would go and put it in the pencil box. Mikey dug his dirty snot rag out of his pocket and wrapped the box in it. We buried it by the big cottonwood tree close to the pond, then carved an "x" on the side of the tree so we wouldn't forget where it was planted. We stood there with our hands on our hips and admired our handiwork.

"I'm so glad I found you, Frankie. I've missed you."

"Me too." This time I let him hug me and felt a strange lump in my throat. "Now you best scoot home before you get in trouble."

He waved goodbye as he ran down the road toward the Johnson's stately farmhouse. I picked up my pace as I headed the other way toward the Wheeler's. Bet I'm in for a tongue-lashing for sure. First day of school and I'm late for chores.

18 Big Rube

The rest of the school year went without a hitch and soon school time ended and another summer arrived.

Mac counted on a huge tomato crop each year. He planted a whole field of tomatoes and hoped a bountiful harvest would put a few extra dollars in his pocket. My job was to weed and hoe to keep the rows nice and clean all summer.

"Watch those rows, Frankie. They have to be straight as an arrow."

After I had to smooth out the dirt and start over a few times, found the trick to hoe the perfect, straight row was to look straight ahead towards the end of the row instead of looking down or checking where I'd been.

Found the Wheeler's weren't big on holidays. Every day was like the other – a work day. Sundays were a short break in the week, but chores still had to be done. So, when the Fourth of July came – my twelfth birthday – I learned to expect the same thing as the year before: nothing.

It seemed no time at all and the tomatoes were ready to harvest. The crop was so plentiful, Mac decided to hire extra help. I talked him into hiring my younger brother Mikey as one of the helpers. A few more kids from school also took the $2.00 offer to pick tomatoes on Saturday. It sounded like easy money, but they didn't know how many tomatoes there were!

One bright, sunny August morning, Mac decided to get his young crew in early before the sun made the day too hot to work in the field.

I was surprised to see "Big Bad Rube" –at least that's what I heard the other boys call her –show up on the field. Ruby wasn't fat, but she was large for her age. Her big bones made her look muscular and tough. She really wasn't bad either; she was just one who would take any dare that came her way. Ruby had bright red hair and flashing black eyes to match her gutsy daredevil personality. She could stare anyone down and not move a muscle. I thought of the day when Gomer dared her to catch and eat a fly. No one thought she could actually catch one, but she did, and down the hatch it went without a blink. No second thoughts, no regrets.

We worked hard all morning and picked many bushels of tomatoes. While picking, I discovered a wonderful horned tomato worm on the underside of a leaf. It was bright lime green with little black spots that looked like eyes on either side. It had a very sharp horn that poked out its backend. The worm was as fat as my little finger and about four inches long. I picked the worm off the leaf and immediately thought of Big Rube. All kinds of fun ideas paraded through my head. I tucked the worm in my shirt pocket and waited. After a few hot hours, Mac announced a break time. Sweaty, tired, and thirsty, we were all ready for a bit of rest and a drink of water.

I pulled the half-crushed worm from my pocket and held it high.

"Who wants to earn an extra two bucks?" I grinned and looked each one straight in the eye, ending on Big Rube. Immediately I had everyone's attention. They saw what I was up to. Ruby flashed her black eyes at me and then eyed the worm with suspicion without a smile or a blink.

"Two bucks to anyone who eats this worm!" I challenged. I'm ready for a little action today. I stared at Big Rube again. Would she do it?

Mikey quickly caught on to the game. He took the worm from my hand.

"Yu-mm-mm..." he smacked his lip and held it close to his mouth. "Look how big and juicy! Bet it tastes really good!" he taunted, "just like lime pie!" He dangled it back and forth in front of Ruby's face.

The worm wiggled in Mikey's tight grasp. I watched Ruby's face. Yep, she was definitely thinking about it. She stared good and hard at the worm, and then tugged at her red braid.

"Come on, Ruby," goaded Mikey, "tell me you couldn't use two extra bucks?"

The other kids entered in the act. "Yeah Rube! Do it. Do it. Ru-by – Ru-by – Ru-by!"

It hadn't occurred to me where I would get the extra two dollars. Mac planned to pay all these kids $2.00 each for the day, but not me. This was part of my daily work which earned me a place to sleep and eat. No money for me. I could probably squeeze it out of my brother Mikey, even if it was a whole day's pay. He'd pay just to see Ruby eat the worm!

Ruby didn't have to think too long; good thing she didn't. She snatched the worm from Mikey's hand, stuck its head in her mouth and bit it off clean. Green goo spewed from the worm and dribbled down her chin. Ruby started to spit the piece of worm from her mouth, looking a little green herself.

"Oh no! No spitting allowed! Chew it up and swallow it – all of it," I prodded with a grin.

"Ru-by – Ru-by – Ru-by," chanted the others, louder and faster.

She gagged, chewed some, gagged again, then swallowed it, and gagged some more. The boys enjoyed the show; some of the girls turned their heads and gagged with her.

"Now, the rest of it!" I laughed out loud. I glanced over Mac's way to see if he was watching. He seemed to be enjoying the whole show and even waved two dollars in his hand, egging on the shenanigans.

With even more gusto, now that I knew the payoff was covered, I coaxed even more. "You gotta eat the whole thing, Rube. Don't stop now!"

Ruby glared at the other half of the green worm still wriggling in her grasp, then at me, then at the rest of the kids. Couldn't quite tell if her face looked green or white. Whatever color it was, she didn't look well, but it didn't stop her. Good ol' Rube ripped off the horn, closed her eyes, took a huge breath, and popped the rest of the worm in her mouth. Didn't even chew. Swallowed it whole. One gulp – gone.

"Open your mouth, Rube. We want proof," someone yelled.

She opened her mouth wide and wiggled her tongue for all to see. Green slime dripped from her chin. She'd done it. Green goo squirted between her yellowed teeth as she grinned to accept her bonus pay from Mac. Funny. She never came back to the farm after that day.

Yeah, Rube was all right. Didn't know a gutsier girl around. My twelfth birthday may have come and gone that summer, but seeing Big Rube pull off that stunt, well, that was the best birthday present I ever got!

C.A. SIMONSON

19 Trouble at School

One day as I neared the school house I noticed three of the older boys circling a smaller kid. They pushed the kid down over and over. He got up, just to be knocked to the ground again. Why didn't he fight back?

"Goody-two-shoes," I heard one say as he laughed and poked and spun him around. He pried off the boy's stocking cap from his overly butch-waxed hair and made the boy beg.

The closer I got, the angrier I got and I didn't even know who it was. It made me mad to see them treat a kid like that! I determined to help the poor boy being twirled like a top. Once I got close enough I recognized it was Mikey – my brother, Mikey! Defend yourself, my mind screamed. He just stood there and didn't do anything.

"What's the matter with you?" I yelled out. "Fight back!"

Then I saw Jesse on the ground in tears. Blood rushed to my head and I swear steam must have rolled from my ears. I was so mad. Where was the teacher? Face red, and eyes ready to pop, I got a big chomp on my fist and ran towards the offenders. Pushed through the circle of boys, grabbed my brother and pushed him out of the way by Jesse. Swung with all I was worth with the other arm and hoped to catch a few faces in the wake. Biting my fist seemed to give me leverage – or courage – or maybe added momentum. It seemed to help somehow. Three against one wasn't quite a fair fight, but I got my licks in.

The school bell rang but we continued to fight. The teacher finally showed up, ruler at her side and fire in her eyes.

"Inside. At my desk. Now."

Two black eyes and a bloody lip later, I stood before a very irate teacher still shaking with anger.

She looked from one boy to the next. "Who started this?" she demanded.

The older boys smirked and winked at one another, then pointed at me. "The new kid!" they all agreed.

"I did not!" I shouted. "They were teasing my bro… I mean, they were teasing Michael."

"Teasing doesn't hurt anyone, Frankie," she scolded. "So I'll ask again. Who started the fight?"

"The new kid," the older boys sang in unison. "He threw the first punch!"

"But they were tormenting him – twirled him around, shoved him down!"

"Not another word, Franklin." She looked at the older boys. They shrugged their shoulders and tried to look innocent.

"B-b-but…." This would not be a fair argument. Did she not see a thing? And my name's Frankie, not Franklin. I looked at her in disgust.

"No excuses. We will not have fights in this school. Off to the corner with you. The rest of you open your readers and get busy."

I stood dumbfounded with my mouth hung open. I could not believe she would let these boys get away with their actions. Defiant, I stared at her.

"Frankie! Now!?" She pointed to the corner.

"I have to go…"

"You have to go straight to the corner!"

"But I really have to go!"

"Not another word, Frankie."

She took me by the shoulders, turned me around and gave a small shove in the direction of the corner.

Head hung low, I faced the wall and crossed my legs to stop the urge. When I couldn't hold it any longer, I didn't know what to do – until I spotted the trash can. I didn't want to wet my pants, and this was the best I could think of at the moment.

I reached my foot as far as it would go until my shoe touched the can. Little by little I nudged it closer to the corner where I stood to relieve myself without too much commotion. Tried to be quiet about it, but all the kids were watching with stifled giggles. My gut felt like it would burst. Pulled the can into the corner and peed. One little girl in the front giggled out loud and alerted Ms. Barnes' attention.

"Frankie!" Her face was crimson. "For that you'll stand in that corner the rest of the day. No lunch, no recess!"

I shrugged my shoulders. What else could I do? Gotta go? Ya gotta go. By afternoon, my stomach growled and I felt my knees grow weak from standing. Felt faint and started to fall over. Grabbed at the closest thing handy to break a fall and made a bunch of noise which attracted the teacher's attention again.

"Frankie, I've had enough of your antics for one day!" She placed a piece of paper in the corner. "Now hold that up with your nose and don't move!"

I thought school would never end that day. After school I confronted my brothers.

"Mikey, why didn't you defend yourself this morning? Did you forget how to fight? Why did you let those big kids kick you around? It made me so mad. They could have hurt you or Jesse!"

"Cuz," he shrugged his shoulders.

"Cuz why? I've never known you not to fight back. You're a good fighter."

Jesse piped in, "Cuz we're not s'posed to fight, Frankie."

"Yea, I know. The teacher said no fighting in the school yard; but there are times you gotta fight. Don't be pushed around or teased like that. Stand up for yourself."

"I know the teacher said not to fight, but that's not what I meant, Frankie. Jesus said we shouldn't fight back," Jesse explained.

"Jesus? Jesus who? Is he one of the other boys?"

"No, silly. We met him at the Johnson's," Jesse said. "Jesus says we should turn the other cheek."

"What's that mean?"

"Well, come home with us someday after school. Then you can find out for yourself."

"Will this Jesus guy be there? Does he live there too?"

"You'll see," Mikey said with a wink and twinkle in his eye.

20 Jesse's Last Christmas

For weeks Mikey and Jesse begged me to come see them at the Johnson's. "Just ask if you can go visit the neighbors," they said. "Maybe if Mr. Wheeler knew we were your brothers he'd let you come," offered Mikey.

"I can't tell him that, Mikey. He thinks I'm an orphan."

"You'd really love it here," wheezed Jesse, his voice hoarse. "Especially on Wednesday. That's a special day." He coughed hard. "Lots of kids come on Wednesday," he coughed again. "Then Ma Johnson tells us a story, and we have treats."

"Yeah, Frankie. They treat us real good," added Mikey. "We like it there. You would too. Sure wish you could live with us. Figure out a way to come, okay?"

Mikey nudged me to a corner away from Jesse. He nodded toward our little sick brother and whispered, "You need to come, Frankie, for Jesse's sake."

Jesse's cough grew worse; he made strange sounds when he breathed. He had been sick again and missed a whole week of school. Ever since that cold night on the fence post, he seemed to get worse all the time. He missed his twin sister too and that didn't help.

One cold day in December, I wound up the courage at last to ask about a visit. Something in my gut told me I needed to see Jesse soon.

"Mac?" I toed the carpet.

"Yeah, Frankie. What's on your mind?"

"Ah... there's a kid at school. He's, ah, well, he's really been sick a lot. Ms. Barnes asked me to take him a book," I lied.

"A friend, Frankie?"

He noticed I dodged his look. Found it hard to lie to Mac.

"Yah. A friend. Can I go? Take him his book?"

"Can't see it would hurt. Just be home in time to do your chores."

I was thankful for Mac's soft heart.

The Johnson's lived close to town on a country corner not far from the school. It was just a couple miles walking distance from the Wheeler's. Figured I could get there and back home with plenty of time to spare; at least, that's what I told Mac.

When I arrived at the Johnson's house, Mikey took me upstairs to Jesse's and his room. Little Jesse lay on his bunk. He was so white and skinnier than I had ever seen him before. Every time he breathed I heard that funny raspy sound in his throat. Jesse looked up at me with sleep still in his eyes, almost like he couldn't open them.

"Hi, Frankie," he whispered, almost so quiet I couldn't hear. He began to cough so hard he could barely catch his breath. Jesse laid his head back on the pillow, exhausted.

"I can't figger it," said Mikey out of earshot. "Soon as the Johnson's took us in, Jesse came down with something. Started hacking hard like he couldn't breathe. Ms. Johnson said it was the 'mon-ya' or something like that."

"Maybe he got too chilled on that fence that night in the cold sleet for so long," I remembered out loud. "Remember how he coughed that night? And kept falling off the fence? We thought he was just playing with us. But, maybe he was coming down with the sickness then." I paused, waiting for Jesse to stop another coughing fit. "...then we slept in the barn on musty hay and he sneezed his head off. All that couldn't have helped."

Ms. Johnson brought up some medicine for Jesse and tucked his blankets in tighter.

"You boys go downstairs now," she said. "Let Jesse rest so he can get better. There's hot chocolate and warm sugar cookies in the kitchen. There's just enough time for a snack before the other children arrive."

"What's she talking about, Mikey? What other children? Do other kids live here?" I questioned.

"No, silly. It's just me and Jesse, and of course, the Johnson's two daughters, Mary and Sarah. The girls seemed real happy to have us come live with them. They like older brothers!"

"But she said more children would come."

"Oh, yeah – almost forgot. Tonight's Wednesday – Bible club night! You picked a good night to visit, Frankie! Jesus will be here too! Maybe you'll meet him!"

Good. Can't wait to see the guy who fooled Mikey into not defending himself in that fight a few weeks ago. He must be very smart to trick my brother not to stand up for himself. Four other kids showed up: three other girls and a boy named Jim.

"Is that boy Jesus?" I whispered to Mikey.

"You're funny, Frankie. No. That's Jim. Jesus will come. Just wait and listen," Mikey whispered back. He had a mysterious sound in his voice and a gleam in his eye. What in the heck was going on?

Mrs. Johnson gathered us all in a circle. They sang some songs I didn't know, and then she said told us to bow our heads to pray.

"Let's invite Jesus to come join us today, boys and girls," she began, "for it's His story we will tell. And don't forget to pray for poor little Jesse. He is very weak today so he's resting upstairs in his bed; he couldn't join us."

"Close your eyes and fold your hands," Mikey interlaced his fingers, "like this, Frankie."

"Aw, this is crazy."

"Just do it Frankie," he elbowed me in the side. So I bowed my head, but only half-closed my eyes. I peeked to see if anyone else was doing the same thing. They were, so thought I'd better too. They looked so serious.

Mrs. Johnson finished her prayer. "Come gather around the crib, children. Mary," she spoke to her daughter, "go get ready. We have a very important story to tell today."

In the middle of the room sat an empty doll crib. I joined the others cross-legged on the floor. Mrs. Johnson picked up an old leather-bound book that looked worn from use. I wanted to hear what she had to say. When was this Jesus guy going to come?

"Long, long ago," she began, "it was decided to count all the people in the land. A man named Joseph took his wife, Mary on a long trip to the town of his birth so they could be counted. Mary was about to have a baby. She told Joseph this was a special baby – a baby straight from heaven."

Mrs. Johnson motioned for her daughter to enter the room. Mary came in dressed in a blue bath robe, her head covered with a white scarf. She carried a naked baby doll. She sat down on the floor beside her doll crib in the middle of the circle.

Mrs. Johnson nodded and smiled at her daughter, then continued, "When Mary and Joseph entered the city, it came time for the baby to be born, but they couldn't find a place to stay for the night. They stopped at an inn and were told the only place left was the barn out back; it would offer shelter from the wind and safety from the wild animals. So Joseph helped Mary to the barn where they made their beds for the night."

My mind started to drift. A night in the barn, huh? I know what that's like – soft, warm hay, musty smell – and Jesse with the sniffles and cough. Mikey caught me staring into space and jabbed me in the ribs.

"Listen up, Frankie. The important part is coming."

I gave him a wink and sat up straight.

"Before long the Baby from heaven was born. Mary wrapped him in swaddling clothes, which is like a tight blanket, and put him in a manger."

Mary took her doll, wrapped the blanket around it, and put it in the doll crib.

"They named the baby Jesus, because He came to take away the sins of the world. Shepherds came to worship him after they heard the angels tell them, 'Peace, good will towards men. Today a Savior has been born.'"

"Boys and girls, isn't that a wonderful story? Aren't you glad Jesus came to be our Savior? He was born to take away our sins. All you need to do is to ask him to come live with you!" Mrs. Johnson smiled at each one.

"Just like I told you," Mikey whispered. "He came."

It was dark when I started the walk home. Mac would be upset that I was late. His missus would be even madder. Probably missed supper again. Didn't care. Had some long and hard thinking to do. How could Jesus have tricked Mikey if he was just some baby doll of Mary's? A doll can't talk. Mrs. Johnson said we could ask Jesus to come live with us, but I wasn't taking home any doll. Mikey mentioned this Jesus stuff more than once to me – like he was a real person, like he could talk to him and everything. It just didn't add up in my head. I had to find out more.

The Wheeler's didn't have anything planned for Christmas and Mac decided I could have a day off from doing chores. Mac even agreed to let me have Christmas dinner with the Johnson's. Ms. Wheeler wasn't keen on me going; she wanted me to chop wood for the evening fire, but Mac bailed me out. Good ol' Mac. Maybe he thought I needed some friends. He convinced the missus he would take care of the wood. Jesse hadn't come back to school since my visit there, so I hoped he was feeling better.

"Frankie, dear! I'm so glad you could join us," Mrs. Johnson greeted me with a hug as she let me into the house. "Run upstairs and tell Jesse and Mikey you're here, and then you boys come to the table; we're ready to eat!"

I never in my life saw such a feast of food! Roast turkey, mashed potatoes, yams, homemade bread and jam, and cold, cold milk. It looked like enough to feed an army, and it was spread over the entire table. There were way more dishes than we ever used for our whole family of nine! I ate and ate until my belly hurt.

"Who wants pumpkin pie?" Mrs. Johnson asked.

"ME!" I said with a shout and felt my face redden at how loud it sounded.

Mrs. Johnson grinned. She handed me a huge slice of pie with loads of whipped cream. "Here you go, Frankie."

This is like heaven. Sure beats the bread, lard and sugar! And for sure beats the slop that old goat Wheeler made me eat. Wish I could live here, I daydreamed.

Jesse had not eaten a bite from his plate and hadn't said a word either. His face was drawn. His skin was very white, his eyes sort of droopy-looking with black circles underneath. He didn't look well.

"Why, Jesse honey, you haven't touched a thing."

"My belly hurts, Ma'am," he whispered in a tiny voice.

My belly hurt too, but only because I ate too much.

"Guess we'll have to pray a little harder for you, won't we dear?" A worried-looking Mrs. Johnson gave Jesse a warm squeeze. "Well, you go rest for a while, and we'll call you when we're ready to open presents."

Presents too? Couldn't believe my ears. This truly was heaven. I wished I did live here. But Jesse was too sick to even care. He pushed his chair back and slowly rose. He looked at me with the saddest eyes I have ever seen, then went in the other room to lie on the couch.

That was my first and last Christmas with the Johnson's—and with Jesse. He never came back to school. On top of pneumonia, he developed whooping cough and a high fever that burned his brain. His sickness took his life a few short weeks after Christmas.

Jesse was laid to rest in the little cemetery on the other side of town. I didn't know he was gone until

Mikey didn't show up for school a couple of days. When he told me what happened, I was sad and mad all at the same time. I had to tell someone that Mikey and Jesse were my brothers. Guy and my sisters were gone – who knows where? – and now it was only Mikey and me.

Mac, working on the tractor by the barn, saw me coming down the road, bawling a gusher-load of tears. He knew it took a lot to make me cry. He ambled toward me and put his large hands on my shoulders.

"Frankie, what's wrong, son? Are you hurt?" He lifted my face toward his to check for bruises or black eyes.

"Jesse's gone," I blubbered, and burst into tears again.

"Jesse? Jesse, who? Jesse Johnson?"

"No," I rubbed my tears with the back of my dirty sleeve. "No. Jesse Larue. My brother," I sobbed. "My little brother. He's dead, Mac. They let him die." My body shook with sobs.

"Your brother?" Mac let out a low whistle and pulled at his beard. "Then Mikey...?"

I nodded and buried my face in his chest and bawled some more. It was now my turn to spill my guts about family matters.

21 The Accident

After Jesse was gone, the Johnson's asked me to come over more often to be with Mikey. Mac was willing, but Mrs. Wheeler wouldn't hear of it.

"Horses to tend and chickens to feed," said the missus. "That's how ya earn yore keep, boy. Not by lollygaggin' aroun' doin' nuthin'!"

Chores would always be there, I mumbled to myself. I often thought back to Mrs. Johnson's story and how she said she prayed for Jesse, her story about Jesus and all. Well, Mrs. Johnson's prayer didn't work too well, did it? But then what could you expect from a prayer to some old doll named Jesus?

That summer, Mac convinced the missus that a little more help around the farm wouldn't hurt, so Mikey was allowed to come over more often to help me. I was glad to have my brother close again.

The sun shone bright the fall morning of the accident. Mac had asked me to load some barrels onto the wagon, then haul them to town. I asked if Mikey could come over to help; he agreed.

"Wow, these barrels are heavy!" Mikey said as we teeter-tottered the barrels over to the wagon. "What's in them?"

"Don't know. All I know is that we're supposed to put them on the wagon so they can be taken to the town dump. Mac wants to be rid of them." We pushed and tugged each barrel to get it on to the wagon. In between tugging and pushing, Mikey talked, and talked, and talked some more. Seemed he couldn't shut up about his special friend and felt I had to know all about it.

I didn't want to hear it. Just didn't get it. Finally told him to stop; didn't want to hear another word. It didn't make sense and his constant babbling bugged me.

"Listen, Mikey, if you want to pretend this Jesus friend of yours is real, you can; I don't care. But I've never met him or talked to him, so I just think you just made it up—like some pretend invisible friend. I think it's only a fairytale Mrs. Johnson put into your noggin'. Besides, Jesus was just the name of Mary's doll, wasn't it?"

"No, no, no, Frankie," Mikey chuckled. "Jesus isn't a doll, and he's not make-believe either. He's a real person – and He's my best friend. He goes with me everywhere I go and helps me with everything I do.

"Well, I've never seen him. He must be invisible or magic, or something, then. I rolled my eyes.

"You can't see him because he lives inside me, Frankie."

"That's just plain crazy talk, Mikey. How can that be?"

"It takes faith, Frankie. You have to believe it in your heart. Remember the Christmas story Mrs. Johnson told the first time you came to visit? Remember how she told us Jesus came to earth as a baby? He was sent by God, his father. He came to earth from heaven to take away our sins for everything we ever did wrong. Jesus came to take my place, Frankie. He died for my sins so I don't have to be punished."

"Sins? You, Mikey? Why would you need to be punished? That's crazy talk too. You haven't lived long enough to do anything wrong."

"The Bible says everybody has done wrong. That means me, and you too, Frankie. So, I guess that means we need to be forgiven. When you can have faith to believe that, Frankie, then Jesus will come live inside your heart too. Don't you see? " Mikey explained.

I shook my head and stared at the ground. No. I didn't see. I didn't want to bother my brain anymore, but I didn't want to make my brother mad either. I was upset with him just the same. It just didn't make any sense. It was crazy talk. Time to change the subject and get some work done. Got to leave this subject alone.

"Oh, shoot, Mikey. I've had enough foolish talk for one day. C'mon. There's just one more barrel to load."

Five barrels had been hoisted and loaded. One more to go, and it had a funny smell. As we heaved it upward into the wagon, the lid popped off. I lurched sideways to catch the lid and some of the polluted liquid splashed out all over my pant legs.

"What is that stuff?" Mikey ran to help upright the barrel and keep more from spilling out. He put the lid back on.

"Phew! It's enough to make me sick to my stomach. Yikes, Frankie!" Mikey pointed at my pants, "Look at your pants! They're smoking!"

Looked like steam or smoke rolling off my pants that were smoldering. The cloth seemed to melt right into my leg. I let out a loud holler as the putrid liquid reached my skin.

"Ow! It burns! It's burning a hole right into my skin!" I jumped up and down and screamed and pulled at my pants to get them away from my leg, but the fabric had already melted to my skin like glue.

Frantic, I pulled at the pieces of my britches to get the burning to stop.

Mikey doused my legs with a pail of water, but it made the material cling even more, burning and stinging my leg in pain.

"It hurts!" I whimpered. "Feels like a hot poker burning a hole through my leg."

I flopped to the ground and rolled on the grass, trying to remove the wet clinging pants from my leg. A big ugly bump started to form on my calf. My leg was red and swollen.

"What do I do, Frankie?" Mikey looked scared as he gawked at my leg.

I groaned in pain. "Go get a gunny sack from the barn."

Took the hay-crusted sack and wiped at my wet, reddened, burned leg. As I did, disintegrated strips of cloth from my pants came with it. Had to get to the house and wash this junk off. Couldn't have the missus see me in my underwear looking like this. Wrapped the gunny sack around my lower body and hobbled towards the house.

"You need a doctor, Frankie! That bump on your leg is turning purple! I can almost see the veins in your leg!"

"Listen to me, Mikey," I blubbered, fighting back tears, "no one can ever know about this. No one. Not Mac, and especially not his missus. I'll be in big trouble if they find out. You go on home now. I gotta get to the house and change before they see me. I'll be okay. Just don't tell."

"Okay, Frankie, okay," Mikey yelled over his shoulder as he ran home, "I'll pray for your leg."

I half-hoped his prayers would work because I was in awful pain. Yet, I doubted any prayer would work; it hadn't so far. May even make matters worse. I stumbled to the pump, washed my leg good as I could, and then snuck into the house through the outside cellar door. Flopped on my cot and hoped the pain would stop. It got so intense, I finally passed out — and wasn't even missed for supper that night.

C.A. SIMONSON

22 Sacrifice

A few weeks passed after the accident, and the huge, ugly bump on my leg remained swollen and purple. Never did tell Mac. It was still painful to touch, but tried not to limp or show any sign of discomfort in front of him or Herb. The five barrels had been loaded on the wagon, but then forgotten in all the commotion.

One dismal Sunday morning I woke up anxious to have some time to myself. Sundays were a day off, of sorts. Still had the normal chores to do, but for the most part I could do as I pleased. My plan was to spend some time at the pond, fish a little, and think hard on all Mikey told me. He just wouldn't give up.

"Frankie," Mac said, "ya never did take those barrels to town like I'd asked ya to. They've been on that there cart for too long now. I want ya to take 'em to the town dump. They're already loaded, so ya can hook the horse to the wagon and haul 'em all into town yourself. The man at the dump will help ya unload 'em when ya get there."

"But today's Sunday, Mac." I grinned and winked at him. "You know the fish are biting." My smile faded fast. He looked me straight in the eye and didn't smile.

"Sorry, son. Ya shoulda taken them into town when you were told. You'll do it today."

Lowered my eyes and nodded assent, but sure didn't want to go to town. The sky was gray and overcast. Dark clouds hung low. The air was so heavy I felt the dampness on my skin. It smelled like rain -

the way it looks and smells before one of those furious storms on the prairie break loose.

I worked with the horses before, but today they were jittery, stomping their hoofs, letting out little whinnies. The last thing I needed was to be soaking wet and have to tug these heavy barrels. I was afraid my leg would give out if I tried to lift them. Well, Mac said someone would help.

The back dirt roads with all the holes and ruts made it difficult for the horse to pull the wagon with its weight. The sky got darker by the minute; I heard thunder rumble in the distance. Storms sprung up quickly on the plains, dangerous ones. I was anxious to get the barrels into town, unloaded and back to safety as fast as possible. It was slow-going, but found the dump and the man who would help.

"Whatcha doin' with these acid barrels, kid? That stuff inside is dangerous! If that mean stuff spilt on ya, it would burn a hole in ya," he said. I nodded my agreement.

Before too long, we were done. I clucked at the horse to go home. The sky looked even more ominous than before as the black clouds tumbled and rolled above. People rushed out of the little church on the edge of town in an attempt to beat the approaching raindrops. Among them were the Johnson's with Mikey and the girls.

"Whoa." I pulled back on the horse's reins. I hadn't seen Mikey since the day my leg got burned. We spotted each other at the same time. He waved and sprinted toward me.

"Frankie! I'm so glad to see you! Come home with us for dinner?" Mikey looked at Mrs. Johnson with a can-he-come look. She smiled, nodded yes, and waved at me. I reached for the lever to brake the rear wheels of the wagon. My leg screamed as I strained to pull the lever back.

"Got rid of the barrels, huh, Frankie?"

Nodded and winced as I hopped off the wagon. "How's the leg?" Mikey half-whispered. Without waiting for an answer, he rushed on a little louder, "It's going to rain anyway, and I've got plenty of stuff to tell you Frankie – say you'll come! Please?"

"More stuff 'bout Jesus?" I rolled my eyes, then kicked myself inside for being such a jerk.

"Maybe..." He tilted his head sideways and grinned, undaunted. He danced a circle around me. "We learned some neat stuff today and heard a great story. Besides, it's Easter today – a real special day. Say you'll come." He gave me a little push; almost caused me to fall down.

"Mikey," I warned and tried to frown, but I was more curious now.

"I know a secret, Frankie," he teased. "Come over to our place and I'll tell you."

Just then a huge lightning bolt flashed across the sky followed by a loud boom not far behind. We both jumped. It made the skittish horse jump and whinny. "Wow! That was close! Listen, Mikey. I need to get the horse back to the barn before it starts to storm. He's too jumpy now. I'll see if Mac says it's okay." I stroked the horse's mane to calm him.

The sky lit up again with such blinding light it was hard to see. The loud crash was even closer than before. It seemed as if the lightning struck at the horse's hooves. The frightened horse bumped hard against me and smashed my bad leg against the wagon. I cried out in agony, and fell to my knees. The horse reared on his hind legs over my head. I was afraid of those sharp stallion hooves that could slice the skin to the bone. I ducked my head between my knees for protection when I heard Mrs. Johnson scream.

"No! Mikey, No! Don't!"

In the same instant, my breath was knocked from me as my brother slammed his body against mine sending us both tumbling. With no thoughts of his own safety, Mikey pushed me away from the frightened horse's hooves and put himself in direct danger. He knew I couldn't move fast enough without his help.

In a blur of motion, I watched as Mikey attempted to roll us both out of the way of the downward thrust of hooves. As he did, his foot got entangled in the fallen reins. He reached to free his foot as the horse landed full force, hooves first on his back. I heard the sickening crack of his bones as they crushed against the rocky road.

Blinding lightning flashed again with another thunderous boom which spooked the horse even more. The terrified stallion took off on a gallop with the now-empty wagon behind him. He stomped over the unconscious boy whose foot was still caught in the reins. Women screamed, and some men rushed after the spooked animal. Thunder, lightning, and the yells of the men only made the horse run faster. I tried to get up to run after the horse, but my bruised leg sunk me back to the ground.

I fell in a heap and held my head, aghast at the horror I was witnessing. This couldn't be happening. It felt like a nightmare. Hoped I would wake up and it would be all better. I felt helpless as I watched

Mikey's limp body bounce like a lifeless ragdoll behind the wagon on the rocky dirt road. Couldn't scream; couldn't cry.

It was over in a few minutes, but it seemed like forever. Mr. Johnson and the other men finally caught up with the animal, but the damage had been done. Mr. Johnson untangled the reins and picked up the broken, bloody, bruised boy. He looked dead, lying limp and mangled in Mr. Johnson's arms. The man listened to Mikey's heart and looked relieved as he heard a small heartbeat. He ran to the doctor's office down the street, but the door had a 'CLOSED' sign on it.

"Someone already went to find the doctor," a bystander offered.

Forced my leg to bear weight and hobbled over to where Mikey lay. Mrs. Johnson uttered huge wrenching sobs as she dabbed Mikey's bloody forehead with her handkerchief. I saw her mouth move in silence as she stroked his head. Probably saying another prayer, I thought in disgust. Skeptical, but really wanted her prayer to work this time though I didn't have faith in her prayers. They didn't work for Jesse. I frowned at the thought.

I was scared. Poor Mikey was so badly broken; blood was everywhere. All we could do is wait for the doctor to arrive. Wait – and pray? I scoffed at the thought.

The doctor worked on Mikey all afternoon, but it was hopeless. He never regained consciousness. Not only was his back broken, but most of his bones were crushed. The doctor said there was bleeding inside and he could do nothing to help him. The life had been drug from his crumpled body.

It was my fault. Mikey had taken my place. His brotherly, unselfish love put his own life in my place. It should have been me, not him. I didn't deserve his love.

Fate missed its mark again, but found another brother as its harsh target. The Johnson's couldn't have paid me to live with them now. Two of my brothers died in their care; didn't want to take my chances. Just wanted to get as far away as possible from this terrible, cruel town of bad memories.

23 Another Pa

Mac let me skip school for the rest of the year after Mikey's accident. Summer sizzled by without event. Even the tomato picking had lost its fun. I was lonesome without my brothers. Worked hard to forget. Felt like I was worth nothing, but farm work had a way of getting one in shape again.

Mac found out about the incident with the acid after Mikey's accident. His approach to my chores took a big turn when he understood why I limped, even though the missus thought I was just lazy. The barn became my sleeping quarters again since I'd grown a few more inches and put on more weight. The fruit cellar was a mite too crowded once all the fruit and vegetables were in store. A couple years flew by as the rhythm of school and chores ran together.

Baling time arrived again and brought with it a strange day that would forever be burned in my memory. The sky was a bright blue that autumn morning. The smell of newly mown hay scented the air and a slight breeze blew through the window. My age, height, and strength improved my skill to sling bales, but my leg bothered and hindered balance. My face turned into a grimace with every twist and throw of each bale. The calf of my leg was swollen to the size of a large grapefruit with bumpy purple and blue veins threaded like worms under my skin. It cramped something fierce if I stretched too far but I gritted my teeth to hide the pain and kept on the job. Herb had noticed. Though I did not voice my complaints, he saw the frowns and heard me wince.

"What's the matter, kid? Where's those muscles? C'mon, put some guts into it."

I gave a half-cocked grin and flexed my muscle at him, turning the other way. He noticed that too.

After a very long, hot and dusty day, we headed back to the house. The bump felt as if it would burst open. It had been almost a year since the accident with my leg. Mac noticed my slight limp, but didn't comment. He looked troubled and deep in thought; furrows creviced his forehead.

He stepped off the tractor with a hitch in his step, took off his straw hat and scratched the back of his head. Then he gave me the most disturbed look I'd ever seen. Reminded me of the first day I met him; when he stared me down at the cow tank. Made me curious, but I knew better than to ask. He would speak when he was ready, and not before.

That night at the supper table, Mac unloaded his burden. I wished he would have told me without his missus there to listen in. It was none of her business in my opinion, but she cocked her head to the side so she wouldn't miss a word.

"A man stopped by here this week, Frankie," Mac said. "Wanted to know all about ya."

"Who'd ask about me?" My hopes peaked. Maybe Guy had found Pa and they were going to get the family together again.

"Some guy from the big city, Ah reckon, the way he was dressed. Ah can't remember if he even said where he came from. Said he's wantin' to come by and visit ya. Claimin' to be yore Pa."

I looked at Mac in disbelief. "Pa came back? Did he say anything about Guy or the girls?"

Mac shook his head. "All Ah know is what he said. He'll stop by tomorrow to pick ya up and get acquainted-like. But Frankie, jest a word of warning. Ah'm not sure what he knows, or who he knows. Jest be careful. Don't think he's the man you knew as yore Pa."

I swear that was the closest thing Mac ever said about caring for me. It made me more than a little worried. I was confused. Who would want to see me?

The whole night I tossed and turned in fearful anticipation; checked the clock every couple hours. Was it excitement – or dread and terror? Couldn't figure it out. I only knew one Pa – the one who left us alone sitting on a fence post that cold rainy night a few years back. The guy who drank away his earnings and caused Ma and the seven of us kids to go hungry. The guy who couldn't hold down a job, the man who beat us. He was the only man I called Pa for ten years of my life. Now another guy claimed to be my Pa? Maybe he was just some guy who saw free help. Maybe he needed a farm hand for cheap labor. What better way than to pick up an orphan kid and say he belongs to you? My mind wouldn't stop. Finally drifted into a fitful sleep plagued with horrible nightmares and monsters.

When I entered the kitchen the next morning, I was fearful of what and who I'd see. The strange man sat at the table with a cup of coffee. It for sure wasn't my Pa; I knew that. Wasn't any relation I knew. Large and rugged, the man was dressed in a new suit and tie, nice, but not too fancy. He seemed okay, I guess. Didn't have a clue and was kind of scared, even if I do admit it. What did this man want?

"Yore gonna spend the day with your Pa," the missus squeaked, sounding a little too gleeful.

"He's not my Pa...." I started, but she spoke over the top of my voice.

"Yore gonna go with him today," she screeched louder, cutting me off. "So be off with ya. Now!"

The large man spoke in a deep calm voice, "We'd best be going. "I'll explain everything, Timothy."

Curious, how did he know my real name?

"Let's go to town and get some breakfast, and then we'll go to the park. I brought you a present," he winked. "Then we can get to know each other better." He nodded at the missus. "I'll have him back by dark, ma'am."

"Don't ya hurries none," she replied without looking at me.

Mr. Simmons was tall: about six feet, four inches, large in stature, but not fat. His eyes were the same strange blue-green as mine – the kind that seem to change colors. I couldn't tell if I had the same color hair; his head was already gray and thinning in most places. He had a silly looking gray mustache. His hands and face were very, very brown like a person who worked outside all the time. I didn't think I looked like him at all.

We had a large breakfast at Fanny's Café in town. Mr. Simmons chatted about his farm outside of Omaha and how grand it was. He tried to act all rich and important; said he had a hundred head of cattle and all kinds of horses and two hundred acres of land. He seemed to know a lot about Dolly and Guy too. It was all very strange. I sat quiet and listened; tried to be polite and answer his questions. My mind felt jumbled up, but not as much as it was going to be. I had no idea what the next few hours would bring. It turned out to be beyond my wildest thoughts.

After breakfast was over, we walked a block to the park. Mr. Simmons retrieved a new ball and mitt from the trunk of his car. "Let's play some catch, Timothy. You do know how to catch a ball, don't you?"

It felt like he was trying too hard to win me over and become my friend. After we tossed the ball back and forth a few times, the strange man pointed to a park bench.

"Let's sit a while Timothy. We need to talk."

He put his arm around my shoulder and guided me to the bench. In the awkward hours that followed, the stranger told me an unbelievable story. He claimed to be my real father and tried to persuade me to come live with him. Said my mother and he parted ways when I was a baby.

"Your last name isn't Larue, Timothy, it is Simmons, and that is Guy and Dolly's surname too. Do you know where they are? I want to find them so they can come live on my farm too."

I shook my head and stared wide-eyed at this stranger. He kept talking, but my mind went crazy. It was too much to take in. I didn't get it. If Mama left him, how did she end up with a drunken bum like Pa? Was this man even worse? There had to be a lot more he wasn't telling me. Why did he show up now and not before? Guy or Dolly never mentioned another pa. But he knew their names – and mine. How could that be? Why now? None of it fit. I wanted to ask, but couldn't. I just didn't buy it. It had to be a lie. All of it. My mind was so busy trying to process the whole idea, I missed a lot of what Simmons said. I was so confused.

"So Timothy, I will be glad to have you come live with me," Simmons continued matter-of-factly. "You'll be a good fit on the farm. I'll be back in a couple of months to move you to my place. You'll like it there. You will see. It's big and spacious with lots to do! Be ready to go when I arrive, because I'll need to get back to the farm without delay. Do you understand?"

I dumbly nodded, but my eyes were vacant. Couldn't believe this was happening.

"All right then," he laughed deep and low and patted my head. He pulled the pocket watch with a huge gold chain from his pocket and checked and the time. "I better get you back to the Wheeler's."

I kept quiet the whole ride back. My stomach and my head hurt from all the jumbled mixed-up thoughts. So, he *did* own a farm. I knew it. And he wanted me to be ready to move? In a couple months? Another Pa? Can't be. And Guy and Dolly too? Did I have no choice in the matter? How did he even find me? I stared out the window and shook my head to clear the fog. Things did not make sense.

Mac wasn't my pa either, but he took me in when I had nowhere else to go. He treated me like a son. He was kind to me. He warned me about this guy, so wouldn't he defend me? What would he think about this plan?

"You are very quiet, son. Are you feeling okay?"

"Just thinking." Kept my face toward the car window so I wouldn't have to look at him. And don't call me son, I thought in disgust. I am not your son. Stared out the window the rest of the way home.

Maybe I should have gone to the Johnson's when they offered to have me move in with them. They thought it would be good for Mikey to have his older brother with him after Jesse died, but Mac wouldn't hear of it. He didn't want to lose me, but now he's willing to let me go? Just like that? What did Simmons tell him? Was he threatened, or did Simmons buy him off? So many questions, and no one to ask. I was so confused. One thing I did know – I was not going to move in with him, Pa or no Pa.

Simmons stopped the car a distance up the road from Mac's farm, but did not turn off the engine. I got out, slammed the door, and started up the drive without looking back, saying thank you, or goodbye.

Simmons rolled down his window and called to me, "Don't forget, Timothy. I will be back soon. Have your things packed and ready to go – all of it."

It sounded like a warning. I turned to look, and saw him smile – a strange, evil-kind of smile.

"Don't forget your ball and glove. They're yours to keep, son." He held them out toward me with that smile frozen in place.

Didn't want to, but I walked back to the car and took them from the man who claimed to be my pa.

"Be ready," he warned again, then rolled up the window and drove away. I glared at the car with a frown on my face until it disappeared in the dust. The gifts in my hand felt like rocks. Don't call me son, I thought bitterly. I am *not* your son. I threw the ball and glove as far as I could into the field.

My steps were deliberate as I walked up the drive to the house, deep in thought and feeling miserable inside. This just wasn't right. Maybe Mac didn't know the whole story. Had to talk to him. I sure had a lot of questions, but it appeared Mac had other things on his mind. The missus was complaining to him that he let me out of doing chores all day. When I started to speak, he gave me a look that said "not now" so I went to the barn. I felt so alone.

This day would be forever etched in my mind as the strangest, weirdest, most rotten day ever.

24 New Headmaster

It was well past harvest the day I went back to school. Mac insisted I go, but it was sad to know both my brothers were now gone.

I drug my feet to the back of the class with the other older boys. Dagnabbit, I thought, trying to ignore the lump in my throat that threatened to choke me, Mikey promised to always be there for me. And now who will have my back? Didn't want to go back to school. Felt I'd learned enough, after all, I was fifteen now. What more did I need to know? Why even go? What was the use anyway? I sat in silence and thumbed through my book. Didn't feel like schoolwork or anything else. I missed my brothers.

All heads looked up as a middle-aged man entered the room. Short, rotund, and bald, he walked over and stood behind the desk.

Where was the lady teacher? Maybe they thought she didn't handle discipline too well, so maybe they fired her. Or maybe she got married. Married ladies weren't allowed to teach in this school.

Mr. Collins almost reminded me of Santa Claus with no hair. Chuckled under my breath at the thought. Even had the little thick round glasses. Collins seemed to have a permanent frown creased into his forehead. Come to think of it, I never did see him smile. His little beady black eyes that peered from beneath his thick glasses were far from jolly. Those eyes seemed to bore right through a guy.

After a week or so I could tell I wouldn't get along with this guy. Stern and strict, he had way too many rules. Me and rules just didn't mix. Proved that once or twice. The older boys enjoyed getting the teacher mad because his face lit up like a beacon. The blood started to creep up his neck until it reached the top of his head like a thermometer. It was a funny thing to watch – unless you were the object of his wrath.

It seemed Mr. Collins had his eyes on me a lot lately, like he didn't trust me or something. It made me wonder. Was it because I started so late in the year? Maybe it was because I limped. Or, smiled at the wrong times. Who knew? He just didn't like me; I could tell. I felt it.

Mr. Collins had a large fish tank close by his desk with all kinds of different colored fish, said they were tropical fish. It was fun to watch the fish when there was nothing to do, or when I didn't feel like schoolwork, which was most of the time these days.

Today was one of those days. Didn't feel like doing a darn thing. We were supposed to be studying, but I was down in the dumps. Missed my brother something fierce. The fish were soothing to watch. Took my mind somewhere else.

Out of the corner of my eye, I noticed Gomer, across the aisle, as he unwound the wire from his notebook. He must have been bored too. He straightened the wire out and made it very, very long. I was intrigued. What in the heck was he up to? He took a piece of gum from his mouth and stuck it to the end of the wire.

"Watch this," he whispered.

The long piece of wire wobbled its way past my desk. I held my breath. The teacher would have his neck if he saw. Gomer always came up with some brilliant idea. He had a knack for pulling a stunt and then would get away with it without ever getting into trouble. Other kids' attentions were drawn to the wire as it sniggled past their desk toward the front of the room.

The further Gomer stretched his makeshift fishing pole, the bouncier the wire became. He maneuvered it, sprung it up and down a little more, until it plopped right into the fish tank.

He looked over at me and grinned. I grinned back and held my breath. He held the wire motionless in the tank, then give a sudden small jerk with the gum to bait the colorful fish. The whole class watched in suspense, first on Gomer and his fishing expedition, then on the teacher, who was engrossed in a book. We hoped he wouldn't notice. Not sure how Mr. Collins missed the wire bounce down the aisle right in front of him, but then, his glasses were thick as the bottom of a pop bottle.

It didn't take long before a fish took the bait. Gomer gave the wire a quick upward tug and flipped the fish right smack on the wooden floor close to one of the first-graders. She twittered and drew her feet up under her as the fish flopped closer.

Surprised by the commotion, Collins looked up from his book. Gomer swiftly pulled the wire back to his desk out of sight.

"Funny little fish," the teacher muttered under his breath. "Didn't know they could jump that high." He got up from his desk, rescued the stranded fish, and released it back into the tank.

Gomer smirked and held his sides. Other kids held their hands over their mouths to keep back laughter. Then Mr. Collins saw the wet wad of gum on the floor.

"Who had gum? We all know gum is not allowed in this classroom! Gomer? Bobby? Frankie? " He stared us each in the eye as he walked to our desks in back.

I looked at the floor; Bobby and Gomer held their tongues. The wadded-up wire made a bulge in Gomer's over-stuffed pants pocket, but Collins didn't notice, nor did he see the wireless notebook on his desk. I felt his eyes on me and his hot breath in my face as he leaned over my desk.

"Frankie. Move your things up to the front seat. I want to keep my eye on you from now on."

I shook my head and tried to laugh it off.

"There's nothing funny here, young man. Now. Get a move on."

Wiped the grin off my face, picked up my books and moved to the front desk – right under the teacher's fat face. Why did I always look like the guilty one? I must have a face to blame. I wondered. My face always turned red when someone did something stupid or silly. I couldn't help but grin at a goofy prank. But it always got me in trouble. Oh well. Who cared, anyway? Mr. Collins and I never did hit it off. Never seemed to get on his good side no matter what.

Then came that strange Thursday that ended my schooldays and my relationship with that teacher forever. It was a very strange day indeed. Math day.

Math was never a good subject for me. I hated numbers. Everything about them seemed fuzzy and didn't make sense. Math didn't interest me at all. So, when it came to numbers and figures, my mind wandered instead of paying attention.

Mr. Collins started to explain a math equation and turned around to write on the blackboard. He looked up and down the blackboard ledge searching for the chalk, but none was to be found. He took off his glasses, wiped his eyes, and put the wire rims back on his nose. He looked in the desk drawer, then back at the blackboard, and scratched his bald head.

I jumped as a small piece of chalk whizzed past my head. It hit the blackboard like a small firecracker and exploded into dust, missing the teacher's head by a couple of inches.

I laughed and turned to see which one of the boys threw it. The three culprits laughed into their jackets and winked at each other. More chalk waited in a row on their desks. I turned back toward the front with a huge grin of my own. Old Gomer and his buddies were at it again.

"Frankie! Did you do that?" Mr. Collins kept his voice low and controlled, but the red in his neck started to creep up his collar.

"No sir," I shook my head in fear. I felt the red creep up my own neck.

Mr. Collins frowned, gave me an evil stare, and retrieved a piece of the broken chalk from the floor. He turned back to the board to write fractions. The redness was almost at his ears.

"Watch this," I heard Gomer whisper behind me as he flung another piece of chalk at the blackboard. It ricocheted off the board, then on Collins' thick glasses, then to the floor. The girls stifled their giggles behind their hands, but the boys roared in fright.

The teacher spun around, squared his pop bottle glasses back on his nose and glared at me. I looked guilty as sin. My face was beet red and I couldn't hold back a grin from ear to ear.

He glared. The crimson was past his neck to the top of his ears. Everyone knew what that meant. Gomer and his crew tried to make this man teacher mad every way they could because they enjoyed the show. If he was even a little bit irritated, his nose turned red. The more he rubbed it, the redder it became. He thought we didn't notice, but the clues were easy to read. When he got angry, his neck turned red. The more irate he became, the higher the red climbed. The blood rushed up his neck little by little, reached his chin, then his ears, until it topped his forehead. His eyes would bug out so far they appeared they would pop. The teacher couldn't hide his fury any longer. It was out for all to see. By that time, we knew someone would be headed to the woodshed out back – or worse yet – would get the ruler in front of the whole class. Somebody would be in trouble for sure.

"Who did that!? I demand to know who threw that chalk. Now!" He stood in front of my desk and scowled at the class, searching each face. Then, his eyes focused down on me.

"Frankie, it was you, wasn't it?"

I couldn't wipe the grin off my face. He looked so funny. I felt my face grow hotter and I knew it had to be red. My eyes were wide as I shook my head no. I opened my mouth but nothing came out except for a nervous laugh. I hated myself for that, but couldn't control it. Things only got worse from there.

Collins threw his textbook on the floor, grabbed the edge of my desk and pushed it up hard with me in it. If he were trying to scare me, he did a very good job. As my desk tilted backwards, I went into survival mode. Frantic, I reached for the first thing to keep me from falling out of my desk—the teacher's ugly purple necktie. I grabbed quick and yanked hard. That action drove the teacher's fat face and beady eyes next to mine. Forgetting the tie still clutched in my hand, I tried to hide behind the desk – which pulled Collins to his knees. His pudgy nose collided with the desk's sharp edge in one swift motion. It was like a living nightmare. Blood spurt everywhere. Girls screamed. Boys shouted, laughed, and hooted. It was a free-for-all.

"Good one, Frankie!" yelled one of the boys.

Horrified, I looked down at the tie still crumpled in my hand, the only thing keeping me in my desk. Mr. Collins crouched on the floor in front of me still pressed up against the desk with a bloody, broken nose. His eyes narrowed as he glared at me. I let go of the blood-speckled tie and fell to the floor beside him. He was going to kill me, I just knew it.

"I didn't mean it," I cried. "It was an accident! I'm sorry."

Collins found his glasses, rose from the floor, and went to his desk to find something to stop the blood. He found a hanky to press against his nose to stop the bleeding and focused his angry black eyes on me. He grabbed me by the shirt collar and yanked me upright. The switch on the wall would soon meet my behind. But then the teacher did something even more unbelievable.

Shaking, I stood face to face with the disgraced teacher. Nervous. Scared. My fist headed toward my mouth, then realized the whole class was watching. Stuffed it in my pocket instead.

He spoke in a slow, low, booming voice. Every word spoken was distinct. Quiet. Stern. He pushed his glasses on his broken nose and pointed towards the door.

"Frankie, you need to leave now." His face and neck were brilliant red all the way to the top of his round head. He was beyond mad. He was furious. It made my heart skip a beat. I was done for.

I stared at him with vacant eyes. I shook my head in doubt. What did he mean? The room was silent as frightened students sat stone still in their seats. Collins' eyes bore into my soul. His voice became louder with every syllable, his face more crimson with every word.

"I said: Leave the school house. Now. Right now."

No one had ever witnessed this level of rage before. Danger was imminent. I was terrified.

I didn't have to be told again. It wasn't my fault, yet the blame always fell on me. It's not fair, I screamed inside. Why me? Mad. Hurt. Embarrassed. Ashamed. Mikey was gone. Jesse was gone. No reason to stay in school. Didn't even bother to get my books or my lunch. Picked up my coat and stomped out of the schoolhouse. Slammed the door behind me. Once outside, I shook all over. So mad. So scared. What had just happened? Why did I always look so guilty? I vowed never to return to that place.

It was before lunch, so I couldn't go home yet. I had to process all that had taken place. Was this real, or just a bad nightmare? I ran to the pond where Mikey and I had made our secret pact and buried it by the tree a few years back. Painful memories flooded my mind of my lost brothers. A tear trickled down my cheek. Why did Mikey have to die? I kicked at the dirt, swirling a cloud of dust around of me. I found the oak with the "x" carved in it, and dug up the old pencil box that held our precious pact of promises.

The stained and wadded snot rag had started to rot that covered the box. I held it close to my chest and let the tears come. I unfolded the rag with tender care. Inside, the piece of folded paper was still there –our pact – our promise. '*We promise to always be there for each other and never leave the other behind because we are brothers. Signed Mike and Frankie.*' Our bloody "x's" proved our solemn oath to the other.

But he did leave me, I grimaced. It's not fair. Nothing is fair. What now? What should I do?

For several hours I sat by the pond and bawled my eyes out. I was mad at Collins. I was mad at myself, and I was mad at Mike for pushing me out of danger from the horse's hooves. It should have been me that died, not him. I was the damaged one. And, I was mad at God. Why did he have to take my brother? Why did he let him die? After all, if there were really a God who loved us like Mikey said, couldn't he have prevented it? I didn't understand. Confused. Alone. Sad. I stuffed the paper into my pants pocket and tossed the pencil box into the pond.

When the sun looked like it was close to setting, I headed home to get my after school chores done. As I neared the farm, I saw a strange truck parked in the drive. Curious. The Wheeler's never had visitors. Then I saw him. Simmons came through the door. I froze in my tracks and a shiver went up my spine. It had been a few months since that fateful day in the park. He said he would come back, and now here he was, just as he said. He wasn't dressed up like before this time. No fancy suit and tie. This time he had on scrubby bib overalls with a flannel shirt. Looked like he'd come straight from the field.

It's true. I knew it. Simmons just wanted cheap farm labor – me. He saw a strong young kid and thought I'd be free help. I'm not his long-lost son. Don't know how he knew my name or my brother and sister, but it didn't matter now.

I saw him stuff a wad of money in his jacket. Was he making some sort of deal with Mac? Was Mac paying him to take me? Unbelievable. How could Mac sell me? I kicked a stone in anger. Simmons would not buy me like cheap labor. I would not be a part of his farm or his life. Mac couldn't make me. Simmons couldn't make me. In fact, I would not even give them the chance to try. There would be no goodbyes for this boy. I bit my fist and kicked the rocky road again. I was mad at the whole world.

Before either of them saw me, I headed in the opposite direction. The Johnson's were out of the question. Couldn't go back to Mac's, and I couldn't go back to school. Needed to get far away from here. Too many bad memories and bad luck. But where?

A lonesome train whistle blew in the distance, and a wild, crazy, daring idea popped into my head.

25 Flight

The air smelled musty and damp. My body felt as if it were moving. Shook my head to clear the cobwebs and sleep from my groggy brain. Took me a few minutes to regain my senses, but then remembered I hopped the northbound train.

That stranger who called himself my pa had been waiting for me in his beat-up truck. Forced me to make a rash decision, but was happy I did. Started over once, figured I could do it again. The freight train seemed like the logical answer. Caught up to the train and hopped aboard an empty boxcar before anyone saw me. Found a good hiding spot towards the back half-filled with sacks of grain and loose hay. It was the perfect spot out of sight and half-way comfortable. I would get off when the train stopped.

Must have slept through all the stops, or there hadn't been any. Couldn't tell what time it was, but assumed it must be nighttime; everything was like black velvet around me. Couldn't see if anything shared this boxcar with me or not. Settled back into the loose, dusty hay satisfied with the decision I'd made. Figured I might as well catch a few more winks before the train came to a stop. The clickety-clack of the train on the tracks made that easy to do. The motion and rumble of the train soon lulled me back to sleep.

It seemed only a few moments had passed when I heard the train whistle screech. The iron horse began to slow, and I saw bright light through a crack in the door. Could it already be morning? Seemed I'd traveled a long while. My stomach growled. Turned my pockets inside-out, and hoped I'd find something, but there was only lint and dirt. Wished I had grabbed my lunch sack when I was booted from school. Was that just yesterday? Seemed like years ago already. I smiled with a long yawn. Wasn't sorry I'd left. Good riddance to them all.

Crawled out of my spot in the corner and waited for the train to slow to a creep. Had to hop off before anyone saw me. No idea where I was; must have journeyed a long way to go all night. I pushed the boxcar door open to a crack to see the surroundings. The countryside looked different than the prairies of Nebraska. More hills, more trees. The smell of spearmint wafted through the breeze. A pang of hunger growled from my stomach to remind me how famished I felt.

Caught a glimpse of an open field and jumped out of the boxcar. My bum leg crumpled in pain beneath me as I hit the ground. Tumbled into a rough roll down the small hillside right into a field of fresh mint. Just beyond the field was a town – maybe a mile's walk. Good place to start a new life. Plucked a couple mint leaves and stuffed them into my mouth. Not bad, but made the empty hole in my stomach feel even larger.

A small grocery store sat on the edge of town. Bins of fresh apples and small bundled stacks of fresh mint sat out in front. My eyes wandered over the shiny red apples and then to the candy sticks in jars inside. Ran my hand over the apples and picked one up. My mouth drooled as I imagined it sweetness in my mouth.

"Can I help you, young man?" a soft-spoken, older man asked. He had salt and pepper hair and a pleasant smile. His blue eyes met mine with the apple in my hand almost inside my jacket. Must have read my thoughts.

I blushed and replaced the apple. Avoided his eyes, picked up another apple and pretended to inspect it. His eyes still on me, I felt conscious of my appearance. Must have looked a mess after sleeping on the musty hay all night. Tried to brush some of the stragglers of straw from my dirty shirt. Embarrassed, didn't know what to say, but knew I couldn't steal from him.

"New in town? Haven't seen you around before."

"Yeah. Just got in," I ventured, looking over my shoulder toward the train tracks. "Looking for work." Didn't want to give too much information. Thought about asking where I was, but that would give me away for sure.

"You need some help here at the store? I'm a good worker and I'll work for food."

"How old are you, son?" he asked.

"Going on eighteen, sir," I lied.

"You're on your own then? Traveling alone?"

"Yes sir. I have no kin," I lied again. "Just me." Hoped he wouldn't ask anything more. Didn't want to explain the whole crazy-awful story of my life to this stranger.

His eyes probed me like a beacon on a dark sea. He seemed like a smart man —acted like he already knew all about me, but didn't prod any further. He smiled a kind, fatherly-sort of smile and gave me a solid pat on the shoulder.

"Tell you what, son. Why don't you go re-stack those apples out front for me? When you're done with that, you can sweep the store. Can you do that?"

"No problem!" I replied with a nod and a grin.

"And, if you want to eat an apple while you're working, go ahead. Help yourself." He smiled and winked. A front tooth with a gold filling sparkled when he smiled. "By the way, I am Mr. Neiman."

By the time I finished with everything, it was time to close the store. Surprised it took that long, but Mr. Neiman had made me stop to take a break at noon. Even brought me a glass of milk and a sandwich. It was hard to believe the good-heartedness of this man I'd just met. He didn't know me, yet seemed to trust me. Mr. Neiman pulled the shades and locked the door. I needed to figure out what to do and where to go for the night. Maybe he would let me work for him tomorrow too.

"Listen, son," Mr. Neiman said as he put his arm around my shoulder. "I don't know what or who you're running from..." he stared into my eyes, making me squirm inside, "and I won't ask you. That's your business. You look old enough to be on your own. Just know this: you are safe with me. I won't let anyone or anything harm you."

I tilted my head and looked at him. How could he know?

"You need a place to stay, am I right?"

I nodded and shrugged my shoulders, avoiding his piercing blue eyes.

"I'm going to ask you straight up, do you have a place to sleep tonight?"

I shook my head.

"That's what I thought. My guess is that you haven't eaten a good meal in a while either —or else you really love apples!"

I dared to look this kind man in the face. He didn't sound angry. There was even a hint of a chuckle in his voice. He gave a huge smile and the sun glistened off the gold tooth.

"Would you like to join the wife and me for supper tonight?"

"Really?" Could I hope for some good luck for a change?

"Well, yes. Really. You did say you would work for food, and I think you've earned it today. Besides, my sweet Elsa is already expecting you."

I squirmed inside when he mentioned his wife, but my stomach demanded attention. Felt like it touched my backbone. I agreed to go home with the man, half afraid of what I would find. Would luck be on my side this time, or not?

C.A. SIMONSON

26 Heaven-Sent

The Neiman's lived in a modest and small, but nice home on the other end of the town. An older couple, their children were grown and gone.

"Elsa, dear. This is our guest, Frankie, the one I told you about earlier. He's a newcomer to the area." He smiled his sparkly-gold smile. "Frankie has been a big help today."

Elsa Neiman greeted me with a warm hug. "I am so happy you came, Frankie." She smiled the way I thought a kind grandmother might smile. She took my face in her small withered hands and looked into my eyes. I felt embarrassed again, felt the red rush to my face. Felt ashamed of myself – yet she didn't seem to notice. Never felt so welcomed by anyone; it felt so strange, and yet so good.

"Come in, dear." She led me into the living room.

Elsa Neiman was kind and gentle like her husband. She was a petite woman with beautiful white hair that gracefully wisped back from her face with warm brown eyes that twinkled. Found it curious how different this woman was from Mac's wife, and how that old goat reacted the first time I met her. How I ever managed to live with them a little over five years, I'll never know.

Mrs. Neiman's soft voice sounded like sweet music, soft and melodious. "Jonathan, I am so happy you brought home your young guest to share our meal! You know how I always cook too much." She let out a small laugh, "I got carried away and fixed this huge roast beef today. Who would've guessed we would have company?"

Mr. Neiman winked at her. She flashed him a smile of love and her face flushed a soft pink.

"Frankie, why don't you get cleaned up for dinner while I help my Elsa put the food on the table?" Mr. Neiman pointed to the bathroom. "Oh, and if the shirt on the peg fits you, go ahead and put it on. We will eat when you are ready."

A real bathroom – inside. When I saw myself in the mirror, it made me shudder. I understood why he wanted me to clean up. What a bum. I was dirty with smudges on my face and stragglers of straw still in my hair. Yet, he allowed me to work in his store all day and didn't say a word about my appearance. The plaid shirt from the peg fit like it was made for me. Washed my face and hands, tried to smooth my unruly hair and felt ready at last to join the older couple at the table.

Mrs. Neiman's face seemed to light up when I came to the table. "Come, sit down dear," she motioned to a chair close to hers.

It was hard to take it all in. Though modest, the table was spread for a feast with sweet corn relish, mashed potatoes with rich brown gravy, green beans, and home-baked bread. In the middle of the table sat a chunk of roast beef with steam wafting from it. Took a deep whiff, closed my eyes, and grinned in eager anticipation of a full stomach. The aroma made my mouth water.

She smiled her approval. "Jonathan, let us thank our dear Lord for sending this angel our way."

Out of respect, I followed their lead and bowed my head. At least I learned that much from my brother

Mike. Mr. Neiman said a simple prayer and thanked his God for abundant bounty and provision and for sending me their way.

Through the course of the meal they didn't ask too many questions about me. I was grateful. Instead they told me about themselves.

"We had two sons, Frankie. That shirt belonged to our second son. He moved out east, and we haven't seen him in quite some time. Our firstborn, David, was killed in the war," her sweet smile faded and her eyes saddened.

Mr. Neiman took over her story, "David wanted to see the world and to have great adventures, so he joined the army. World War II broke out a few months after he finished basic training. He was shipped overseas and had served only a few months before being fatally wounded." Mr. Neiman's voice cracked.

I nodded. Waited.

"Started our little grocery store when I was a young man, only a couple years older than you, Frankie. Then, me and my sweet Elsa got married and started a family. The town grew up around us. We always hoped one of the boys would take the store over as theirs. But one went to war, and one wanted to travel."

"I think he wanted to get away from this town," Mrs. Neiman said. "Went out west, we think. Said he wanted to see the ocean. We haven't heard from him for over two years." She dabbed at the tear that trickled over her pink cheek. I hope he is all right, but only the good Lord knows."

Lines of intense worry and pain crinkled the soft face of Mrs. Neiman. She bore the weight of loss and loneliness. Yet, she still had contentment in her eyes. Curious.

"Oh," she blushed. "Listen to me – going on and on like a silly old woman." She took a deep breath as if to shake away the past. She sat in silence for a moment. Mr. Neiman patted her hand and we waited. Her mood brightened and she smiled at me. "Frankie, I'm just glad you're here! I hope you like fresh apple pie."

I nodded with a big grin and jammed another forkful of mashed potatoes into my mouth.

"And I hope you like the room I've prepared for you," she continued. "You know, it's not an accident God brought you into our home tonight. He knew just what I needed today."

Puzzled by her words, I questioned her with my eyes. She gave me her warm grandmotherly-kind of smile again that made her eyes twinkle. It was the same kind of smile Mama had when she understood how my heart felt before I ever spoke a word.

"God knew how lonely I've felt since our boys left home. Today was our Timothy's birthday, and this was his favorite meal. And when Timothy left home..." her voice faltered and trailed off. "It was just too much right after we learned David was killed." A far-away look clouded her eyes as she thought of a happier time. Silence filled the room once more. It made me uncomfortable, but thought it best not to ask questions. Mr. Neiman patted her hand with gentleness and waited. She regained her composure and continued.

"Well, anyway, when Jonathan told me a young man would share our table and our home tonight, I knew right then God still cared about me. He showed me His love through you, Frankie. You are the angel

God sent to remind me that He knows and cares how I feel." Mrs. Neiman searched my eyes with such intensity it made me fidget. "You remind me so much of my youngest boy, Frankie. Your eyes, your blond hair, your build. Such fiery eyes you have; you could pass for my own Timothy."

I cleared my throat to get the crazy lump out of it. Took a drink of water to hide my discomfort. Stared at my plate and refused to look her in the eye.

"What's hiding behind those eyes, Frankie?"

I couldn't speak. Didn't know what to think. What did she mean? She searched my eyes for an answer. It was the second time today I felt my soul was an open book. This kind woman melted a layer of hardness from my heart in a matter of a couple hours. She seemed to really care about me, just like her husband. Maybe someday I could tell her about my life. She would listen and encourage, not condemn or blame. Maybe someday I could pour out my heart —maybe trust someone like her with my secrets. Maybe. Someday.

Mrs. Neiman started to clear the table for pie and I finally found my tongue.

"My name is Timothy too, Ma'am. Frankie's just my nickname."

27 New Hope

The bed felt as if I were lying on clouds. I nuzzled my head into the soft pillow and yawned. Never had I felt a bed so soft or covers so silky. I took a deep breath of the sweet mint smell that permeated the room through the open window. The curtains flapped in the warm breeze; the stars even seemed brighter tonight. Maybe it was just this northern sky, but the stars seemed bigger – like they were trying to give me a message. Fluffed the pillows and stuffed them under my head. Never would I even think to ask or imagine something this great.

Mrs. Neiman's words troubled me though, like a huge puzzle with pieces missing. Her comments rolled over and over in my head. "You're my angel sent by God," she had said, sent to ease her loneliness and pain. "God used you to show me His love," she said. Those words churned in my heart and sunk deep into my soul. Wanted to believe I was the answer to someone's wishes or prayers, but how could that be possible? Wondered if I could ever feel God's love like she did. Could I ever believe in a God who really heard me or knew me? Could I dare to believe He loved me? After all I had been through? Before I drifted off to sleep, I dared to pray, "If anyone's up there, somehow show me." Little did I know, my prayer was already being answered.

"Another stack of pancakes, men?" Mrs. Neiman asked, setting down a huge platter.

"This is about the best breakfast I have ever had! Thank you so much, Ma'am. For everything."

She beamed and dished me up another plate.

"Don't forget your husband," Mr. Neiman feigned pity, then pulled at her apron tie. "By the way, Frankie, I have great news for you. My friend, Joe over at the mint farm, needs some help for a few weeks. Would you be interested?"

Tilted my head back and eyed him under raised eyebrows as I devoured my second round of pancakes and maple syrup. Washed it down with a glass full of milk. Before I could answer, Mr. Neiman continued.

"Oh, he'll pay you for your work, Frank. No worries there. He'll give you room and board, too."

I nodded my understanding. Guess that meant my claim to the soft bed was unlikely. At least wouldn't have to worry about a place to sleep and food to eat. Hmmm... Remembered thinking the same thing before and lived to regret it.

"Good. Then it's settled. We'll go meet Joe as soon as you are finished. Oh, and Frank," he put his hand on my shoulder, "I still want you to sweep out my store every night if you will. I'll pay you, too."

Mrs. Neiman handed me a small bundled package on our way out. "I wish you well, Frank," she smiled and stroked my cheek. I felt my face grow hot under her hand. "I'll pray for you every day and I want you to know you're always welcome at our home." On impulse, she gave me a quick, warm hug; it brought back happy memories of Mama. Almost choked up, but managed to thank her for her kindness and we were off to the mint farm.

The mint farm was two miles outside town. It was Joe's mint fields which bordered the Neiman property. Joe supplied the grocery store with all the fresh mint Mr. Neiman wanted. The main commodity, mint oil, was produced on his farm.

The normal introductions were made and times of work agreed upon. Mr. Neiman bid me goodbye and reminded me to stop by the store later that evening. Joe walked me to the boarding house where a few other workers lived.

"This is your room, Frank," he said. "As long as you work for me, you won't have to pay rent."

I nodded my agreement.

"Get settled in then. When you're finished, come to the mint shed. I'll get you started on your first job."

Not bad. In fact, it would do just fine. Sure beat the barn or the cot in the cellar. The room was nothing fancy, but sufficient: a single bed and a small dresser on one side of the room by the window. The other side held a chair and table to read or write with a small lamp for light. On top of the table lay a very large, old, worn Bible.

I sat on the edge of the bed and untied the bundle from Mrs. Neiman. Inside was a very neat stack of folded work shirts and a couple pair of jeans. Figured they were her son's as they appeared to be my size. I put the clothes away in the dresser. At the bottom of the package was a small sack and something wrapped in foil. Smiled to myself. "Cookies and banana bread," read the note, "for my 'angel'." Even though we only met the night before, I knew Mrs. Neiman was going to be my favorite lady.

Found the crumpled paper in my dirty jeans pocket which had traveled with me for the last two days – my

brother's and my blood-stained pact. I smoothed it out
as much as possible, then on impulse, opened the
Bible and placed it in between its thin pages. There, I
thought. Now it's safe. Grabbed a couple cookies and
stuffed them in my mouth, then headed to the shed
where Joe waited on me.

The first job was to find and pick the most tender,
mint leaves. On the way to the field, Joe told me the
youngest leaves were the best for making oil; the older
leaves made the oil bitter. It was one of the largest
fields I'd seen – even bigger than Mac's tomato field.
Looked like I was the only worker here today. Not
even a big Rube to tease to pass the time. The job
itself wasn't hard, just tedious.

After I finished my work in the mint field each day,
I walked the couple miles to Mr. Neiman's grocer to
sweep the store, according to our agreement. He
seemed to trust me, and soon gave me other jobs to do
as the mint harvest slowed down. I stocked shelves,
and priced food. I enjoyed working for Mr. Neiman.
He was good to me. I liked having a place I could call
my own, to be by myself, no one to bother or ask
questions.

Later in the year, when much of the work was done
in the fields, Mr. Neiman offered to let me make
deliveries for the store. Some of the richer folk liked to
special-order their groceries and have them delivered
right to their homes. I didn't get it – why couldn't they
just come to the store like everyone else and buy their
supplies? But Mr. Neiman said this was a unique
service he could offer and if it made folks happy, he
was glad to do it. Who was I to question? Besides, I
got to drive his old truck to make the deliveries across

town. It was fun learning to drive that old stick shift Dodge. It also brought in a few extra bucks in tip money when I packed the groceries carefully and got the orders correct.

Though I delivered food whenever anyone wanted them, Thursdays turned out to be my most favorite delivery day.

Beatrice Quincy was a kind lady with a very big heart. She was an elderly lady who lived by herself in the ritzy part of town in a huge, beautiful house. She placed her order every week like clockwork; wanted it delivered the same time each Thursday morning.

The first time I met her at the service door, she seemed surprised that such a skinny young lad, as she put it, would bring her such heavy sacks. She must have thought I looked malnourished or something and took pity on me. She always had a sandwich waiting for me when I finished unloading the groceries. She kept my supply of cookies well in stock too. Thursdays were well worth the drive and the work of hauling all the groceries she ordered. Don't know what she did with all of them, but she always had three or four bags full delivered. I counted the days until Thursday arrived and tried to keep in mind to pack lighter sacks.

C.A. SIMONSON

28 Invitation

Mr. Neiman stopped me one Saturday night as I was about to leave the store.

"Frank, would you like to come to dinner tomorrow with Elsa and me?"

My head nodded before I spoke. The meals at the bunkhouse were okay – but they were nothing like a great home-cooked meal.

"There's one little catch, son," Mr. Neiman winked at me. "We'd like for you to join us at church first, then come over to the house afterward for dinner." He raised his eyebrows and smiled his wide smile, making the gold tooth gleam.

I scratched the stubble on my chin and eyed him, but didn't answer right away. Wondered what they would do there? I'd never been to a real church service. I shrugged my shoulders and squinted a little.

"What do you think, Frank? Elsa will make your favorite – pot roast."

I looked down at my clothes. They weren't what I thought church-going clothes would be. "Well..." after a long pause, "I'm not sure I'd fit. I've never been to a real church."

Jonathan Neiman chuckled. "Don't worry how you look Frank. Just come as you are." Mr. Neiman scratched his head as he thought out loud, "but, if it would make you feel more at ease, I think my Elsa could find you a good white shirt in Timothy's drawer and maybe even a tie."

I scratched my head as I thought about it.

He could tell I was hedging. "I think Elsa made a chocolate cake too," he persuaded.

The more I thought about the dinner that was to follow, I couldn't resist. Gave him a grin; he knew my weak spot. It was agreed then. We would meet in front of the little white church in the morning.

I was there bright and early, with Timothy's white shirt buttoned tight around my neck. Tie was crooked, but it was on. Nerves tense. Didn't know what to expect. Hoped I looked alright. Almost took the big Bible, but decided not to. That Book made me a little leery; didn't think I should move it or touch it much — after all, it was a holy book. It was doing a fine job guarding my precious paper, so I left it alone. Not sure why I was afraid of that book. Maybe church would answer some of my nagging questions.

Jonathan and Elsa Neiman arrived a few minutes after I did. Mr. Neiman held me at arm's length and checked me over. He helped straightened the tie then put his arm around my shoulder like he did the first time we met in the store and gave me his gleaming smile.

Elsa Neiman's face beamed and patted my hand. "You look fine, son. Real fine. I am so glad you joined us today," she said.

Followed them half-way towards the front, and eased onto the hard, dark oak pews. Soft music played in the background as people entered and sat here and there. The church was small and modest: pews formed a semi-circle around a speaker's stand in front. Bright sunlight played prisms on the floor and ceiling and bounced through the beautiful stained glass windows. The music had a magical lilt; stuck in my head. Found myself keeping rhythm with the beat and the strum of the guitar. The melodic voices drew me – wooed me to participate. I listened, and liked what I heard.

"Love lifted me, love lifted me; when nothing else could help, love lifted me." The words encouraged me; but at the same time, tugged at my heart.

Mrs. Neiman looked my way and smiled her sweet smile. I smiled back. Reminded me so much of Mama. She was so nice to me; felt like she loved me like her own son. Mr. Neiman too. It felt good to be welcomed and cared for by them. I settled back and enjoyed the music in this new place.

After the choir sang, the preacher walked behind the stand. He opened his Bible and started to read. Everyone stood, so I did too. Noticed many people followed along from their own Bibles. It seemed everyone had respect for the words being spoken. So quiet. So reverent.

The preacher spoke of God's love and said we should show that same love to our neighbors – not just the ones we know or like, but to everyone. "Everyone is our neighbor," he explained, "and if God loves them all, then so should we."

That was news to me. Did that mean I had to love the pa who left us kids to fend for ourselves? Or that mean, cruel witch who treated me so bad at the Wheeler's? Did that mean loving the Johnson's who let both my brothers die? The thoughts spun in crazy turmoil in my head.

"You can't give that kind of love on your own," he continued. "You don't have the tools or the ability. You need supernatural help to love some people, isn't that true?"

People nodded. Someone said, "Amen." Now that made more sense. Straightened up in my seat and leaned forward to hear him better.

At the end of the sermon, the minister asked anyone who wanted that kind of love to come forward to the front for prayer. He said God would put that supernatural kind of love in our hearts if we just asked. Oh. I get it. Wasn't that same message the Johnson's tried to preach at me? Made me uncomfortable. Felt hot around my tight collar. I unbuttoned the top button and loosened the tie.

Mr. Neiman saw me shake my head. He gave me a kind fatherly look, and put his arm around me. "You okay, Frank? What do you want to do?" he whispered.

"Nothing," I croaked.

"You sure?"

"Yah – I'm fine."

"Okay, Frank," he patted my back, "okay."

Hung my head and slumped back in my seat. Not going to get me to walk to the front. Huh-uh. Not me.

The dinner after church was painfully quiet. The food was great, but I wasn't hungry. Too many thoughts rumbled through my mind. Played with my food; pushed peas to the edge of my plate, sipped my milk, and re-mashed my potatoes. I was troubled and it showed.

"Did you enjoy the service, Frank?" Mrs. Neiman probed.

"It was okay," I mumbled. Couldn't look them in the face.

Mrs. Neiman cleared the table with my plate of half-eaten food. "How about some chocolate cake?" she put her hand on mine, "Your favorite, Frank."

I withdrew my hand and stood. "No. Need to get back to the bunk. Thanks for dinner."

Had to think. Couldn't talk. Too many things to sort out. I was confused. My heart beat hard inside my chest, but didn't know why.

C.A. SIMONSON

29 The Angel

Tried to make sense of the preacher's words. They repeated over and over in my head: *forgive – love – be thankful.* I was thankful for my new-found friends, I argued with myself, and for the jobs at the mint farm and the grocery store. Things started to change for the good since coming here, had to admit that. Even though this time of year brought back memories of my lost brothers again, had to admit there was a God in heaven to thank. He had shown me a special kind of love through the Neiman's I never knew anywhere else.

The Neiman's didn't give up easily. They invited me to church every Sunday, always with the offer of dinner included. Mrs. Neiman knew my soft spot; I loved her desserts. Sometimes attended just to get the Sunday meal afterward. I really did enjoy the services too. They intrigued me, wooed me, pursued me, but couldn't persuade me. Wasn't ready to admit how I felt yet. Something held me back.

Thanksgiving was little more than a week away. Decided it was time to attend church again and offer thanks to a God I wasn't sure was there. When I scooted into the pew beside Mr. Neiman, he raised his eyebrows and gave me that sparkly grin. He patted my shoulder affectionately, handed me a song book and pointed to the words. The songs had started to grow on me. Even knew a few words and sang along.

The choir's song drew me in; I closed my eyes to listen without distraction. Then a beautiful, clear voice began to sing crystal melodious notes that sounded like an angel.

"Amazing grace, how sweet the sound...." Her sweet soprano voice –unrestrained, pure, and clear – heavenly-sounding.

> *"...that saved a wretch like me. I once was lost..."*

She was as beautiful as her voice. Sweet, young – maybe my age? Chestnut hair, sparkling brown eyes. She looked my way as she sang. Her face was radiant, her eyes sparkled.

"...but now am found, was blind, but now I see."

The words melted their way into my heart. Her face glowed as she finished her song. It seemed she smiled at me and I felt a shiver travel up my spine.

She stepped off the platform, and walked to a pew a few rows in front of us. She smoothed her light blue dress and sat down, curling her long hair behind her ear. It glistened as rays of sun danced upon it. Almost envisioned a halo crowning the head of this beautiful angel.

Not much of the sermon the reverend preached landed on my ears that morning. Too entranced by the angel so close. Her every move, every tilt of her head captured my mind. Every time she looked at her Bible or wrote down a note; I missed nothing. Her attention was on the preacher and the words spoken. I couldn't stop looking at her, reliving the look she gave me, and the smile sent my way. She had smiled at me, hadn't she?

All through the message, I devised ways to meet her after the service. I had to get her name. As soon as the "Amen" was said, people stood to leave. People milled around me, wanting to visit and mingle.

"Frank. So good to see you again." "Frank, welcome back! Thank you for coming."

I had to find that girl.

"Frank, did you enjoy the service?"

I nodded, smiled, and answered in clipped words. Felt cramped. Wanted to go. She was going to get away before I could meet her. Had to find her. Finally, the people around me moved enough to exit the pew. Looked everywhere for her, but she had vanished.

I had just seen my very own angel, and now she was gone. I was determined to find this girl and get to know her.

Church had just taken on a whole new meaning.

C.A. SIMONSON

30 Surprise Meeting

Monday morning found me at the store earlier than usual. Mr. Neiman caught me whistling as I swept the store. Hoped the week would go quick. Couldn't wait for the next Sunday so I could see my brown-haired angel again.

"Mind if I sit by you again next Sunday?" Tried to act casual, but my face told on me.

"Of course, Frank. You can join us any time." He eyed me sideways. "Dinner too, I suspect?"

"Oh, I don't need dinner," I caught his hesitation and explained, "I just want to attend church again – with you." He nodded with curious chuckle.

"Well, you know you're always welcome at church and in our home, Frank. By the way, you know Thanksgiving is this Thursday. Elsa and I would be happy if you would join us."

Mr. Neiman picked up some onions and potatoes as he spoke and placed them in a brown bag. "Here," he handed me an empty bag. "Mrs. Quincy needs her delivery early this week. Help me pull the rest of these supplies together, then you can drive them over to her." He produced a very long list: fresh fruit and vegetables, nuts, canned goods, dry foods. I couldn't believe all the food this one lady ordered – almost six boxes full of groceries. What was she going to do with all of it, feed an army? With the truck full, only one delivery would be made on the east side today.

Mrs. Quincy met me at the service door.

"Frank! Come in. Thank you for making the delivery earlier this week. I have so much to do!" She headed toward the oven while talking over her shoulder. "Think the cookies are ready. Want one?"

I followed her into the kitchen, boxes in my arms. The smell of sweet ginger and molasses cookies permeated the air. My stomach grumbled.

"Could you stay a while and help me, Frank?"

She assumed I would answer yes and kept right on talking. "I'm almost finished with my cookie baking marathon. This is such a busy season. My niece, Annie, came to help me. Oh, land sakes. Put those boxes in the pantry," she pointed towards the second door on the right. "Annie will put the food away if you can stay and help unpack the groceries after you bring them inside."

Figured I could at least do that. Mr. Neiman wouldn't care. Nodded my agreement and took a deep breath of the wonderful ginger cookie aroma as the cookies were placed on the counter to cool. Unloaded the third box in the pantry but still hadn't seen any girl. Then I heard a soft, sweet voice behind me.

"You must be Frank. Aunt Bea said she would have you help me unpack these heavy boxes."

That voice. Could it be? Spun around so fast, almost became dizzy. My mind spun even faster. It was her! My brown-haired angel right in front of me! Her beautiful brown eyes smiled and waited for me to say something. Felt awkward. Time stood still. Stood there and gawked, drunk with her youthful beauty, her flawless skin and perfectly-shaped rosy lips and sparkling eyes. Couldn't find the right words to put in my mouth. Cleared my throat, but no sound came out. Felt the heat rise in my cheeks as time ticked away. Knew my face was red. Turned to pick up some more cans and cleared my throat again.

She giggled and wrinkled up her small pixie nose. She held out her hand, "Let's start over. Hi. I'm Anne. It's so sweet of you to help me."

I took her small hand in my oversized one and shook it. "Hi," I muttered. Felt so dumb. Excused myself to gather the rest of the boxes from the truck.

"Okay. I will put the cans in the food closet. You can lay the fresh food on the table," she said.

She looked different in her blue jeans and sweatshirt. Her chestnut hair, pulled back into a pony tail, bounced when she moved. She looked delighted that I stayed to help. My heart tried to pound its way out of my chest.

"Aunt Bea says you're the best delivery boy she's ever had. You always get her orders right and nothing is ever broken or spilled." She bubbled as she talked. "Says you're a hard worker. Reliable and honest. That's very commendable, Frank."

"Just doing my job," I mumbled. Heat rose in my cheeks again.

"And a mighty fine job at that, I might add," she chuckled, tossing her ponytail in the air as she tilted her head and winked at me.

Kicked myself inside. Felt like such a dummy. Had to think of something smart to say...

"What in the heck is your aunt going to do with all this food? Feed the world?" Oh, that sounded brilliant. Kicked myself again.

"We're making Thanksgiving baskets," her eyes sparkled. "And, no, silly. We won't feed the world, but we will feed some poor and hungry folk around town! A few needy families will get a basketful of food, plus a batch of Aunt Bea's great homemade cookies. I love to come help because it's such a wonderful way to show God's love! Don't you think so, Frank?"

Hmmm...yeah, I nodded. "Sure," I said out loud.

Anne put her hands on her hips. "Okay, Mr. Frank," she commanded in a playful tone, "now we need to set things aside for the baskets." She started to hum a tune in that same pure, sweet voice I heard in church as she worked. Helping her was my dream come true.

The boxes were unloaded all too soon with food in neat stacks awaiting their assigned basket. Thought Mr. Neiman would wonder why I was gone so long to make a delivery. Yet, I didn't want to go back to work. Wished this could last all day.

"Come on, Frank, let's go get some of Aunt Bea's warm ginger cookies before she packs them all away! They're the best in the world!"

Her ponytail brushed my face as she glided past me toward the kitchen. The sweet jasmine scent of her hair made me dizzy. Still hadn't said much to her. My heart thumped so hard, it threatened to pound its way out of my chest. Never felt like this before.

"Come on kids," Mrs. Quincy motioned. "A fresh hot batch is ready!"

I followed Anne to the kitchen counter like a love-sick puppy. She hopped on a stool and patted the one beside her. Mr. Neiman wouldn't mind if I shared a cookie or two before I left, I convinced myself.

Mrs. Quincy set a plate of hot cookies on the counter. "Isn't Annie kind to come help an old woman like me, Frank? She's such a good girl – and helpful too. Don't know what I would do without her help."

Anne blushed ever so slightly making her cheeks flush a beautiful pink.

"Frank?" Anne questioned me with her eyes.

Felt my face grow hot and red. My heart melted with warmth at her look.

"Would you stay a little longer and help me put food baskets together? It would go much faster if we work together!"

Cleared my throat with a loud noise, and pawed the floor. "I need to get back to the store." What was I saying? I wanted to stay around as long as possible!

"Oh, please, Frank," Anne pleaded, as she made a little pouty face, "I would love for you to stay..." She blinked her pretty eyes at me.

Mrs. Quincy laughed out loud. "It's already taken care of, kids! I called Mr. Neiman and he agreed to let you help us the rest of the day, Frank. He knows it's for a good cause, and it would be grand of you to help Annie pack all these baskets. You would be a big help in delivery of these food baskets too. You will help Anne deliver these baskets to the people, won't you Frank?"

I grinned widely, and shoved another cookie into my mouth. "I wouldn't pass it up for the world."

Anne let out a quiet giggle and clapped her hands. "Good! I'm so happy! Let's get started!"

Life was good. My heart felt as if it would burst with gratitude and joy. I had found my angel!

31 The Note

Anne and I delivered twelve baskets full of food to needy families around town. Anne giggled at that fact.

"Twelve baskets full, Frank. We had just enough food for twelve baskets. Isn't that something?"

"So?"

"Twelve, Frank. That has lots of meaning – just like in the Bible."

No, I didn't get it, but that was all right. I enjoyed being with my brown-haired angel. She was next to me and we were together. That is all that mattered, so I nodded my head as if I understood.

I drove and watched Anne deliver the first few baskets to the needy people. She bubbled over with enthusiasm as she interacted with each one. Her joy was so contagious, I just had to get in on it. She was having too much fun by herself. Besides, the baskets were too heavy for her to carry, I convinced myself. I'll be a gentleman and help her. As she presented the basket at the door, some people seemed overjoyed and couldn't say a word, some laughed out loud, others were at the point of tears, full of gratitude.

I have to admit it was a lot of fun doing this kind of thing with her. She called it something else, like being a Good Samaritan or something.

I took Anne back to her aunt's house with a promise to see her again soon. My heart was full as I traveled home.

Thanksgiving dinner a couple days later at the Neiman's was better than I could have hoped for.

Stuffed myself fatter than the turkey on the table. I enjoyed my friendship with the Neiman's, and they seemed to enjoy mine. They were like grandparents I might have hoped for.

"Will you join us at church again this Sunday, Frank?" Mrs. Neiman smiled as she served me a large piece of pumpkin pie.

"You bet!" I answered so fast it made both Mr. and Mrs. Neiman stare at me with curiosity. Then they looked at each other and smiled. I grinned and felt my face grow red. Couldn't wait to get back to church. I had to see Anne again. Of course, I had a lot to give thanks for too —for all my good fortune.

Sunday came and I arrived earlier than usual. Hoped to catch Anne on the way in so we could sit together. Service started with the normal song service and still there was no sign of her. I waited by the door until most of the songs were over, but didn't see her go in. Perhaps she came in the back, I reasoned. Lingered a while longer, then finally went in and sat near the back where I could keep my eye out for her if she slipped in. Mr. Neiman shot me a few curious glances during the sermon, like wondered what I was doing in the back. During the whole service, I kept watch on the door, waiting, hoping to see her, but she didn't come. Where could she be? It didn't seem like her to skip church, especially on Thanksgiving Sunday. I needed to see her again. I wanted to find her, and talk to her.

I had to wait until delivery day and hope Anne was still at her aunt's. Mrs. Quincy lived on the far side of town and I had no car of my own. After a century of waiting, Thursday rolled around. I threw together Mrs. Quincy's supplies, not taking the usual care to package her things in neat order. Her delivery was not quite as large as last week, just two bags. Several other stops were on the docket, but they could wait. I had to make this delivery a priority — had to see my angel again.

Trotted to the door with the two bags under my arms and rang the doorbell. A couple minutes passed with no answer, so I knocked, perhaps a little too hard and waited. Finally, I heard footsteps. Anxious to see Anne, I felt butterflies in my stomach. Hoped Anne's smile would be the one to greet me at the door, but it was Mrs. Quincy.

"Oh Frank! Come in, come in. I'm so happy to see you. Are you hungry? Do you want a sandwich?"

Her manner seemed strange; I always came on Thursdays to deliver food. Strode past the counter to put the packages in the pantry like I did last week, and quickly scanned what I could see of the living room for Anne. My heart beat faster as I recalled my surprise meeting with her the week before. Was she still here? Why did my insides feel so jittery?

"Mrs. Quincy," I tried to calm myself, "is Anne here?"

"Why, no, dear. She went back home. She doesn't live here, you know; she just came to help me with the Thanksgiving baskets last week. She always comes to do that for me. Didn't Annie tell you?" Mrs. Quincy replied. A small smile snuck across her wrinkled face. She leaned towards me and cupped her hand to my ear. "You know," she whispered, "that girl couldn't stop talking about you. It sounded like you both had a great time last week. I even think she might like you."

My face turned red and hot as the heat went up to my ears. At the same time, a spark of hope fluttered in my chest and my heart skipped a beat. But, I also felt disappointment. I hadn't even gotten to say goodbye. "Where does she live? I would like to see her again."

Mrs. Quincy chuckled as she placed a cold-cut sandwich in my hand. She motioned me to sit and eat. "Well, I'm sure you could go visit her if you want to travel a couple hundred miles. You see Annie makes a special effort to come help me at Thanksgiving time. She loves to bake and she has compassion for the needy. That girl is so big-hearted. She just loves to give from her heart just like her mother, my sister."

Mrs. Quincy paused a moment in reflection. "She's gone now...Anne's mother. Passed a few years ago, so I try to give my Annie some mothering when she's here. Think that's another reason she loves to come."

My heart and hopes sunk. "Oh," the words barely came out. "Well, could I write her?" I had to get in touch with my angel somehow. Couldn't let her slip away that fast. "Um...want to thank her, you know?" I blushed, avoiding her eyes. "...you know. For last week?"

Mrs. Quincy's eyes lit up and she smiled with a knowing look. "What a grand idea, Frank! Anne would love that."

"Could you give me her address?"

Her eyes widened as a light seemed to go on in her head. "Wait here, Frank, I just remembered! Before you go, Annie left you something. She knew you'd come today to deliver food and wanted me to give it to you. Silly me. I almost forgot. Excuse me, I'll go get it."

Mrs. Quincy ambled to the other room and was gone a while. When she returned, she held a small white envelope in her hand.

I took the note, thanked Mrs. Quincy, and rushed to the truck. Anxious to see what was inside, I jumped in the cab and tore open the envelope. The scent of Anne's perfume tantalized my nose.

"Dear Frank," it began. *"You were so sweet to help deliver all <u>twelve</u> baskets with me last week. It was fun, wasn't it? And even more fun to share the love of God with all those needy people. It blessed me more than it did them, I think.*

I was very sad I had to leave without saying goodbye to you, Frank. Even though I knew you for just one day, it was great. Feels like I have known you forever. It was my intention to stay all week and help Aunt Bea with Thanksgiving dinner. My father planned to come join us, then take me back home. Then I got a call from the hospital saying my dad was very sick. I had to catch the train home right away to be with him. I am thankful he is better now.

It was great to meet you, Frank. Hope to see you again sometime.
Happy Thanksgiving.
Until then…Anne."

I flipped the envelope over and over, and looked on the backside of the paper. No address? She forgot to write her address on the envelope? I had to know where Anne lived so I could write her back. I ran back to the house and knocked hard on the door again.

Mrs. Quincy flew open the door with a worried look on her face, "Are you alright, Frank? Is something wrong?" she eyed me with concern.

"Sorry to bother you, Mrs. Quincy, but I need Anne's address. I must get in touch with her. She forgot to write down her address! Do you have it?"

"Oh." Her voice sounded befuddled. "Of course, dear," she smiled. "Sit. I'll look for it." She moseyed to the counter and rummaged through an over-stuffed kitchen drawer until she found her address book. I couldn't sit; bounced on one foot, then the other until she found the address. She scribbled it on the used envelope and handed it to me.

With the treasured information in hand and a smile on my face, I rushed out the door anxious to get back to my room so I could write my angel. "Thanks Mrs. Quincy," I yelled behind me as I bounded to the truck, "See you next week!" All the way to the bunkhouse the words tumbled in my brain; I had to search for just the right thing to say.

I sat for a long time at the writing table in my room that night. The words seemed jumbled up; couldn't quite figure how to get my thoughts on paper. Most words got tossed out before they were written down. Didn't want to sound mushy or bold, but somehow had to tell this girl – my angel – how much I wanted to talk to her. How? What could I say? What words would let her know what my heart felt? I never wrote a girl before. Heck. I never even wrote a letter before.

"*To Anne...*" I began. No, that didn't sound right, had to be more than that.

"*To my sweet Anne...*" No, too mushy. This was going to be hard.

"*Dear Anne...*" Hmmm...guess that will work.

32 Soul Mate

"Dear Anne, I went to church to find you on Sunday. I so hoped to see you there. I was sad when you didn't come, but sadder when I learned why you had to leave. I enjoyed our time together, too. Delivering the <u>twelve baskets</u> was fun. You remind me some of my sister. She's close to your age, I think...."

Could only think of a few more things to say. Thought I'd better ask about her father. Sealed the envelope and got it ready to mail the next morning. I hoped she would write back. I didn't have to wait long for an answer. Within a week, a letter came back to me.

"Dear Frank! How pleased I was to hear from you! How sweet of you to ask about my dad. He's much better now; I'm so relieved. It will be Christmas in a couple weeks, and we want him to be fully recovered for that. Aunt Bea is coming to visit us.

You didn't tell me you had a sister! Tell me about her! Where does she live? Do you have other brothers and sisters? Where do your parents live? I want to know everything about you, Frank."

Went on to tell about her Thanksgiving, her father, her school. Anne was the youngest in her family. Her brother and sisters were all married. Her mother died when she was young. Her Aunt Beatrice stepped in as the mother figure in her life, although it was long-distance. She told how Christmas was special to her; how her family celebrated the season, caroled and ice-skated in the park, dinners, and of course, the Christmas story. It brought back my own Christmas memories – and the lack of them.

And so the letters began. I had mentioned my sister without thought, so felt I needed to explain further. Didn't intend to share my life with anyone, but it felt safe to tell Anne. Once I wrote about my sister Dolly, I had to tell about my older brother, Guy. Writing about my two older siblings opened up a floodgate of repressed memories; but I wasn't ready to tell all yet. My little brother Jesse died right after Christmas, and Mikey's accident happened a year later. This time of year was still tough to go through. Writing about it seemed to help though, and maybe, just maybe, in time I would be able to tell her everything that happened with my family.

> *"Dolly sounds like a wonderful, sweet person, Frank! I do hope to meet her someday."*

Little did she know – I didn't even know where Dolly was, or if Josie or Gracie still lived with her. By now Dolly would be in high school, if she went back to school. I didn't know if Guy was even alive or where he ended up. They were the only ones left. My younger brothers were gone, and that story was too painful to tell.

Church became a good habit with Sunday dinner following. The Neiman's enjoyed my company and I enjoyed theirs. It wasn't even a question if I would attend Christmas Eve service with them.

The minister preached how Jesus came to earth as a baby, with the knowledge that he would someday be a sacrifice.

"...and his name shall be called Wonderful, Counselor, Prince of Peace, the Mighty God, the Everlasting Father."

My mind drifted back to the story of Christmas Mrs. Johnson told at Kid's Club years before. It seemed like ages ago. Back then, I thought Jesus was the name of the doll in the story. Laughed at myself for that thought.

The scripture tonight struck a nerve, reviving awful memories again. *Everlasting Father?* I shook my head and stared at the floor. The only father I'd ever known beat us, drank, and gambled our family's money away; the one who sat us on a fence and abandoned us. It was hard to imagine a father who loved unconditionally. Mac had tried his best to be like a father, and he did seem to care for me. My mind whirled. But then again, he was ready to give me away to another man who claimed to be my real pa. Didn't know how a real father should act towards a son. If anyone acted fatherly towards me, it was Mr. Neiman. He was kinder than anyone, and never asked for anything in return. He demonstrated the kind of love that drew me in and allowed me to lay down my defenses. I thought about the service all the way home. I had to tell Anne.

"Dear Anne, Tonight I went to a Christmas Eve service. I heard once again about the father who sent his son to earth. You know, the first time I heard this story, I didn't even know who Jesus was," I confessed. *"I thought he was another kid down the block. Later I thought Jesus was a doll in the story. I have learned tonight that he came to bring peace to the earth. Guess I'd like to know more. What the preacher said about an everlasting father really caught my attention...."*

I poured my heart out about the dad I had known as a kid, then about Mac and about Simmons, who claimed to be my real father. Then I told Anne about Mr. Neiman and the love he had shown me. Real peace? No. Too many rough times in my life. I opened up to Anne like never before. Needed someone to spill my heart to and she seemed a safe place to unload my grief. Maybe it was easier because it was on paper instead of face-to-face. It was simple to let the pen dribble out the words, good or bad, and hope Anne would understand.

I put the letter in the mail and waited. I was so anxious to hear from her, and she always wrote back.

"Dear Frank, Aren't you glad God is a Father to us? That's what it says in the Bible. He knows our every hurt and cry of our heart. He wants to bring us peace: to fill the empty hole in our hearts. The Bible even says he takes our tears and keeps them. Your tears, Frank. They are like a fragrant offering to Him. He knows every time you or

I've cried –every time your heart hurts. I am so glad He takes my heartaches and pain away –as far as the east is from the west! All I had to do was ask him."

The Bible seemed alive for her. I so wanted that too. I wanted the assurance she had. She jotted a few scriptures at the bottom of each letter. She made the Bible mysterious enough to make me want to search for clues myself. I was intrigued to know what the Book on my night stand had to say for me. Anne captured my attention in my heart and in my soul.

Anne could not have known how deep my hurts and confusion were, but my brown-haired angel always seemed to know just the right words to soothe my mind. She didn't realize how each letter persuaded my heart to believe more every time she wrote. Yes. My curiosity was piqued. I was enticed to know more – more about her, and more about the God she believed in so deeply.

Anne was faithful to answer all my letters, and I looked forward to each one. They gave me the answers I needed to hear. They were my lifeline. Over the months and miles, our relationship grew. She understood me, but did not judge me.

I had found my soul mate, and I was falling in love.

33 Mint Muddling

The letters continued through spring and summer filled with memories and questions on my part, and full of caring encouragement and answers from my angel.

Joe gave me more responsibility in the mint fields. I helped plant, irrigate, pick, and bundle the mint. After a hot, back-breaking day in the field, I was ready for bed and a good night's rest.

"Tomorrow, I'll teach you how to muddle mint. That will be your main job for the next few weeks," Joe informed me. There was another lesson to be learned on this mint field.

The next morning, Joe sent me to the fields to select the youngest, most tender leaves. The first step was to prepare them by washing in a basin, then to damp-dry them.

"Mint's purpose is to be bruised and crushed," Joe said. "It's the only way to extract the sweet oil from it. The process of muddling is to bruise and press. The essential oils must be released without smashing the ingredients. Press firm and slow," he demonstrated with the pestle as he gently compressed the leaves, pressing ever so lightly with his hands. "The idea is to press hard enough to release the precious sweet oil without destroying the mint leaves. Here, Frank – you try." Joe stepped aside and handed me the pestle.

I laid my full weight into the pestle and pressed down. My face grimaced into a frown as I pressed harder and harder concentrating on the pestle circling the large vat. Years of pent-up emotion were released with each swirl. Soon, the leaves lay pummeled into a dark green slimy mass. Joe stood and watched in silence as I crushed every ounce of life from the leaves.

To me, the first batch of mint appeared ready. I presented it to Joe, proud of my accomplishment. He tasted it, pursed his lips, and spit it on the floor.

"Bitter, Frank, very bitter. It should be sweet to the taste. Bruising the leaves the correct way brings out the sweetness of the mint; battering makes it bitter and sour." Joe took the green slime and tossed it into the garbage. "This batch will come out of your pay this week."

I shrugged my shoulders a little and smiled sheepishly.

"Here, Frank," he placed a couple mint leaves in the palm of my hand. "Clap your hands together." I clapped. "Smell the mint? Feel the oil on your hand? You only need a small amount of pressure to release the oils. Try it again. Press and twist and remember, use the light touch, Frank. This time – please be more gentle."

I began the process and Joe placed his big rough hands over mine. "Gentle, Frank, gentle. Do not bash or pound, okay? I want you to bruise the leaves, not bludgeon them."

The more I muddled the mint, the more my mind muddled the past. It felt like I had been the one under life's pestle these past years. I was the one being crushed, my feelings bruised, my family pummeled. Had to remember to keep the few good times in my head, but the bad times seemed to far surpass the good ones. All the unjust cruelties kept re-playing in my head like a broken record. I knew deep down I had to forgive, but it was too hard to do.

After a full day of pressing and twisting, there were only a few ounces of oil to show in return for all the soreness in my body. My shoulders burned and my back ached. Couldn't believe how much I hurt. The sweet smell of mint that was once so refreshing was now nauseating. My body screamed to lie down and crash to sleep, but I had to write Anne first and tell her about my day.

> *"My dear Anne, today I learned how to muddle mint. It's tough to extract just the right amount of sweet oil from mint leaves. Today was a rough day. My body aches like I've been bruised and beaten.*
>
> *My mind and spirit feel crushed like the leaves, under the enormous weight of circumstances and problems.*
>
> *Do you think anyone ever cared about what happened to me? No one was there when my dad beat and whipped me, or threw our mom and kids out of the house. No one cared when Mac's wife treated me so cruel – not even Mac..."*

I wrote of the other nagging thoughts in my head – better end my letter on a good note.

> *"So Anne – thank you for being there for me. Somehow, I believe God sent you to be my angel. You have helped me understand so many things. I'm glad you listen and respond. Your letters are my lifeline. I sure*

wish I could see you again. I would love to talk to you face to face. You're my sweet Angel. Love, Frank."

Stretched my arms to relieve my aching muscles and looked around the room. My eyes were drawn to the Book on the nightstand – the silent Guardian of the pact.

"That Book that holds every answer for your life," Anne wrote, *"it's like a treasure chest. Dig into it, Frank. Search for its treasures like you would hunt for hidden gold! Let the words speak to you, Frank – let them speak right into your soul!"*

I picked up the Book with care and ran my finger over the old, worn leather cover. Someone must have used this Bible a lot. As I flipped through the onion-thin pages, it fell open to a page marked with a purple ribbon. The scripture was underlined in red with handwritten notes in the margin.

"Surely he hath borne our griefs, and carried our sorrows: yet we did esteem him stricken, smitten of God, and afflicted. But he was wounded for our transgressions; he was bruised for our iniquities..."

I read it over and over again and again: *"stricken... smitten... wounded...bruised....* The note scribbled on the side read, *"Jesus understands: he had a hard life too. He was beaten and bruised for me."*

"*...smitten of God and afflicted...*" Even his father rejected him! I didn't understand and I was too tired to try.

I laid my tired body on the prickly feather ticking of the old cot, and thought of those words as I drifted off to sleep.

"*... Surely he hath borne our griefs, and carried our sorrows.*"

But does he care about me? I wondered.

C.A. SIMONSON

34 Burnt Cookies

As I continued to write Anne, my relationship with her Aunt Beatrice grew as well. She looked forward to our Thursday visits as much as I. She always had something ready for me to eat to persuade me to sit and chat a while.

Throughout the summer she found other reasons for me to visit. I washed her windows, mowed lawn, trimmed bushes, did odd jobs and ran errands. Didn't mind. I liked Ms. Q, the name I grew fond of calling her. She was a kind old lady who was very nice to me. Of course, she paid me extra cash too, which was icing on the cake.

Over the months, I grew to love Ms. Q like a grandmother and learned much more about her. She encouraged and spurred me to be the greatest person I could be. Tried my best to please her. I would have done anything she asked.

"My husband was once the CEO of a huge corporation in the city, Frank," she told me one day. "The company employed many people and took him on business deals all over the country. He made thousands of dollars and gave me everything I ever wanted. But his work of such long, hard hours left precious little time for home – or me," she confided.

Mr. Quincy died at a very young age, which left his wife alone in a huge, beautiful estate with lots of money, but no heirs. Ms. Q never remarried, but instead busied herself with social affairs, clubs, and humanitarian efforts, pouring her life into helping others. She had the means to help and she had the time.

"It's been almost twelve years now since Thomas passed. That's why I am glad Anne comes so often to visit. It helps me to feel less lonely, and together we make people happy. After Thomas died, Anne's mother, Helen, came to stay with me for a couple weeks. Let's see, Anne would have been almost four years old at that time. They came to visit often. I fell in love with that little girl just like she was my own. Annie held the key to my heart," said Ms. Q. "When my sister, Helen died, Annie was just ten. It was only natural that she look to me to fill that void."

Mrs. Quincy said Anne came to visit as often as possible, even though she lived a few hundred miles upstate.

The sun was shining brightly that beautiful July morning. I was almost ready to start my regular Thursday run to the north side. I packed Ms. Q's groceries with love and care: light-weight sacks, all the fruit together, the bread and bakery goods separate from the rest, and the canned goods on the bottom of the bag. On impulse, I located one of her favorite magazines and a small box of candy, and slipped it in the bag with the rest.

My mouth watered thinking about the fresh home-baked cookies I knew Ms. Q would have ready for me. She always said she didn't bake them just for me —she just liked to bake. I smiled to myself. Then why did I always end up with almost all of them to take home? She knew all my favorite ones too. I sure had grown to love this little white-haired lady.

Her place was scheduled last because she always had a sandwich or some kind of food prepared. It was her plan for me to stay and chat a while. Today though, something tugged at me to go to her place first. It felt urgent. Didn't know why, and didn't question my gut, just headed the truck toward the north side of town. As I neared her house, something felt out of place; couldn't put a finger on it, but it troubled my heart.

Saw the smoke a block away. Stepped on the gas. Had to hurry. Hoped it wasn't Ms. Q's house, but when I neared the house I could see ominous, black smoke creeping out the partially-opened kitchen window. My heart beat faster. I jumped out of the truck and barged through the door. No proper 'service delivery' knock today. Smoke billowed from the kitchen; the room was hazy.

"Mrs. Quincy," I yelled. "Are you here?" Rows of neatly stacked cookies garnished the counter, but what I smelled wasn't fresh-baked cookies, it was acrid and burnt. Found the source of the smoke and opened the oven. I yanked the burnt tray of blackened cookies from within and threw them in the sink. Sirens blared in the distance. Someone must have already called.

"Mrs. Quincy! Where are you?" My eyes burned; felt as if I would choke. Coughing and sputtering, I ran to the living room in search of my elderly friend. As I gasped for clean air, I stumbled over what I thought was a rug on the floor. Squinted with teary eyes and had a sick feeling as I realized I had tripped over the crumpled body of Ms. Q She was face down on the carpet, unconscious.

Frantic, I grabbed the afghan from the back of her rocker, threw it over her face, and gently cradled her in my arms. Had to get her outside. Felt dizzy, walls were spinning; had to get us away from this smoke. The fire trucks and paramedics arrived as I came out the door. They ran to meet me. I carefully laid my friend on the grass, then dropped in a heap, hacking the smoke from my lungs.

They checked Ms. Q for vital signs. Her breath came in shallow gasps; her skin was ashen. They asked me so many questions I didn't have any answers for.

"We'll be with you as soon as we finish with the lady," one man said.

"Will she be okay?" I rubbed my stinging eyes.

"How long was she lying in the smoke?"

"I don't know, I just got here. The house was full of smoke. I found her on the floor in the other room. I hurried to get her out as fast as possible."

"How did it start?" another asked as he checked my blood pressure.

"I think she was baking cookies. Must have fainted," I guessed.

"Well, you did the right thing. We need to get her to the hospital right away. She is stabilized for now, but still unconscious."

I wanted to ride with her but wasn't allowed. I followed in my truck. I needed to let Anne know – she would want to know – she would want to be here. Did I dare pray for a favor from God?

"Please God, let her live…"

Would He even hear me? Does He even know who I am?

"Please, God, please..." I begged. "I'll do anything if you just let her live."

35 The Wait

The hospital waiting room seemed stark, cold, and uncaring with its white walls and hard linoleum floor. Fumbled through the magazines and tried to read, but couldn't. Anne needs to be here. What should I do now? "Do you care?" I half-prayed as I stared out the window toward a cloudless sky.

I stood as the doctor came toward me from the Emergency Room.

"Are you related to Beatrice Quincy?"

"Ah, no. I'm just her grocery delivery guy."

"Well, your fast thinking saved her life, young man. You got her to fresh air just in time."

"Will she be all right?"

"She inhaled a lot of smoke, so she is still in grave danger. She mentioned someone named Anne. Do you know anyone in her family named Anne?"

"She is my girlfriend," I nodded. "I mean, Anne is her niece, almost like a daughter."

"Is there anyone else in the family? Husband, children, sisters or brothers?"

"No," I replied, "just her niece, Anne."

"She had a mild stroke. Must have collapsed and hit her head when she fell. The smoke only complicated matters. She could have easily died, son, and burnt up with her house had you not arrived when you did. See if you can contact Anne. It may be the last time she'll see her aunt. It's going to be touch and go for a while and she will need special care," the doctor stated matter-of-factly. "For now, you can do nothing more. Go home."

Couldn't write Anne— she needed to get here as soon as possible. Decided to send a wire. Even if she could come right away, it still may take a couple days.

I tried to visit Ms. Q in the hospital whenever I could pull away from my job. She looked so frail. She was too weak to talk a lot, so I didn't stay too long. Just wanted her to know I was there.

A nurse stopped me at the front desk on my way out of the hospital the third afternoon.

"Are you Frank Larue?"

"Yes?"

"Mr. Larue, there has been an accident."

I froze in my tracks. "An accident?"

"Yes, a Miss Anne Sharp. She was admitted this morning."

My heart screamed. I stared at the lady behind the desk but my mind spun a thousand miles the other direction. Not another one. God! Not another one. You took away my Mama, then one by one, you've taken them all away. Everyone who I ever loved – Jesse, Mikey, Mrs. Quincy. Please, not my Anne – what do you want from me? Please, God, not Anne!

"Sir. Are you all right, sir? Your face looks white as a sheet."

Focus. Big breaths. I looked at the lady and managed, "Is she okay? What room?"

"Room 278. She asked if you had been here today. Glad we caught you before you left."

My heart raced as I hurried towards the elevator. I need her, God. Please. I can't make it if you take another one.

"Rooms 210-230 to the right; rooms 240-280 to the left," read the sign. The halls seemed to stretch on forever. Anne's room was almost at the end. I braced myself for what I would find, quickened my steps and then stopped short at the nurse's station. The door to Room 278 was closed.

"Nurse? Can I go in? Room 278?"

"No. Doctor is with her now. You will have to wait," she answered curt and stiff.

This can't be happening. I held my head in my hands and cried silently to the One I hoped could hear me. "God, you have to help her. Please don't take her from me."

Paced the hall, got coffee, sat on a chair, and then paced the hall some more. What was taking so long? I could only imagine the worst – maybe she was unconscious, or broken, or ...or worse. Couldn't bring myself to accept that. "Please God – I need my Anne."

The door finally opened, and the doctor left. I peeked around the door to find my angel sitting up in bed with a huge purple goose egg under a bandaged head.

"Annie? What happened?" I hurried to her side.

"Oh, Frank! I'm so glad you're here." She held her arms toward me. Big tears swelled in her eyes, then streamed down her cheeks.

I sat by her side and stroked her silky hair, wrapped her in my arms, gave her a gentle hug, and kissed her bruised forehead. I wanted to soothe her fears. I wanted to tell her all would be fine.

"Are you okay?"

She rubbed her sore forehead where I kissed her, and forced a weak smile. "I'm fine." She gave a deep sigh. "I'm just glad you're here now. I drove all day and all night and got too tired. Almost here, I sideswiped a fence post, went into the ditch, and bumped my head on the dash. Because it's my head, the doctor wanted to watch me for a few hours. It's just a little bump. I'm okay. I'm just worried about my Aunt Bea. What happened Frank?"

Her smile told me she was glad to see me, but it was also strained. She was worried about her aunt. I told her what I knew.

"I'm so glad you were there, Frank. You saved her life! She could have died."

The nurse entered the room. "The doctor says we can release you, Miss Sharp. You need to watch the bruise on your head for swelling, but you'll be fine. The doctor wants you to go home and get a good night's sleep."

"What about my aunt? Can you tell me?" she squeezed my hand, her eyes anxious.

"You have to talk to the doctor in the morning. For now, go home and rest."

Anne latched her arm in mine as we strolled to the truck. On the drive to the Quincy estate, I opened up much more than I planned. She was so easy to talk to, even face to face. Felt like I could share anything with her.

"I was afraid I was going to lose you too, Anne." I confessed. "I even prayed – me, of all people. I prayed God would save your life. I was so afraid you would be next."

"What do you mean, next, Frank?"

"Everyone I've grown to love or gotten close is gone, Anne. God's taken them away – or something has. They've either died or left."

I found the courage to tell Anne how my mother died, how our pa left us, and then about my brothers, Jesse and Mike. I told her some of my fond memories of when we were kids.

"Mike talked about his 'best friend', Jesus, every chance he got, and I made fun of him, Anne. I called him names. I'm so ashamed now. I honestly didn't know who Mike was talking about. Even when I made fun of him, he didn't stop telling me over and over about the One who lived inside him – the Friend, he said, who was closer than a brother. The friend who never left him. I took offense at that Anne. After all, I was his brother. Who could be closer than me?

But, I've come to grips with a lot of that since I've met you. I understand more. I'm not mad anymore, just sad. When I met you, you became the one bright spot in my life. I was so afraid God would take you away too. Annie, I couldn't stand to lose you, too."

Anne stroked my hand and looked deeply into my eyes. "My dear, dear, Frank. I'm so sorry. I didn't know. Things will get better now – I promise."

C.A. SIMONSON

36 Answers?

Anne grabbed my hand and squeezed it tight as we walked into Aunt Bea's room the next morning. The elderly Ms. Q looked so still and frail in the sterile white room. She blinked at us through partially-opened eyes.

"She'll need constant care once she goes home," the doctor had told Anne. "We can arrange for a nurse to come each day for her medical needs, but someone must be with her at night as well. She will need help and lots of patience, care, and understanding. Even then I cannot promise she will fully recover. The stroke may leave her with partial paralysis."

Anne listened in silence, then let out a huge sigh.

"You can see her now," the doctor continued. "Think about the options. You will need to make some decisions regarding your aunt's future."

"Anne...you... came...." her voice trailed. We had to lean close to hear. "I'm not sure... what happened?" She fingered the bed sheet, confused. Her worried dim eyes scanned the room. Her hand shook as she touched the IV in her arm. "Last thing... I knew... cookies in the oven." She reached to pat her chest. "...then my chest....ooohh...." she groaned.

"Yes, Aunt Bea. I'm here now. Shh. Don't speak," Anne stroked her arm. "I will take care of you." Anne smoothed back her aunt's silvery white hair and spoke in a soft voice. "We'll let you rest now and come back a little later, okay? Before we go, can I pray for you?" Anne slipped her hand around her aunt's hand, and then grabbed mine without waiting for an answer.

"Dear Lord," she began.

Mrs. Quincy was too weak to refuse or resist. Her eyes were closed.

"Please help Aunt Bea to get better. Thank you for sending Frank to save her life. Please give her your divine strength, and thank you so much for giving her a second chance to really know you. Amen."

Mrs. Quincy's face was wet with tears. Pretended to scratch my eye before anyone saw the tear slip down my face. Anne's full attention was on her Aunt Bea. She wiped her aunt's face and kissed her weathered cheek.

"I love you Aunt Bea."

Ms. Q looked at Anne with moist eyes, but couldn't speak.

Curious Anne thought God sent me to 'save' her Aunt Bea. Never thought of it that way. Her prayer puzzled me, but now wasn't the time to ask what she meant. Her aunt apparently understood, and the words had touched her heart.

On the way home that day, I just had to ask.

"I heard you ask God to give your aunt a second chance to know Him. I don't know what to think. Who could be a better person than your aunt? She does so many wonderful things for people, gives her time and money to the poor. Surely, God must love her."

"Oh, God does love her, Frank. He loves her more than I do. And He loves you and me, and well, everyone. God proved His love. God loves us all so much He sent His Son to save us, so that we can know Him. He wants to be our very own personal friend – just like he became a friend to your brother. We don't have to be good enough, or think of how much good we can do, or how much we can give to the poor. It doesn't matter who we are, rich or poor, famous or unknown.

God loves us unconditionally, and wants everyone to believe in him and in His Son. Aunt Bea needs to simply believe and love Him, not try to buy His love or do things to earn His love. Do you understand?"

I nodded but and shrugged my shoulders. Maybe I understood a little, but I was still confused.

From the moment Aunt Bea first saw Anne, her strength began to return. The doctor said she still had a long way to go to recover from all the smoke she inhaled. Anne agreed to stay with her aunt until school started in the fall.

Glad my angel was going to stay a while. Still had a lot of questions, and plain and simple – I liked her close by.

That night alone in my bunkhouse, I sat by the table with the huge leather-bound Bible in front of me. I pondered all the events in my life since I arrived in this small Wisconsin town. Some of my puzzling questions about life seemed to be getting answered. Mrs. Quincy didn't die, and it appeared she was getting better. Anne came into my life and God apparently kept her safe when I thought she was in danger. The Neiman's had become my dear friends – almost like family. My job treated me good and there were people who seemed to care about me. Things had definitely begun to turn around in my life since the day I muttered that first simple prayer on the train, "If you're really up there...."

Maybe God was up there and was finally helping me find the answers I needed. Maybe He even really cared about me. Or maybe, I had started to listen at last.

C.A. SIMONSON

37 Nightmares

After a week in the hospital, Aunt Bea was ready to go home. Anne and I had cleaned up the mess and got the house back in order after all the smoke damage. She was glad to finally be back in familiar surroundings. She flipped through the stack of magazines as she sat propped up with pillows on the couch.

She continued to improve with Anne's good care. It was wonderful to have Anne so close. Her home-cooked meals every night soon became the norm. Found every reason possible to show up at the Quincy estate: had to check on the women, offer help, see how Ms. Q was feeling, make deliveries, – after a while, I ran out of excuses. Just wanted to be near my brown-haired angel. After a short while, my actions became a little too obvious.

"I see the way you look at her," Ms. Q said with a wink and a slight smile. "You adore her. It's written all over your face, Frank."

Felt my face get hot and red. "You can tell?"

"Of course, dear," she chuckled. "You would do anything for that girl. It shows. And if I know my Annie, she knows it too. I've watched you two together. She may even feel the same way. Never let it get old, Frank."

We did enjoy each other's company. It felt, well, natural. Like it was supposed to be. We talked, laughed, and joked. We were comfortable around each other. Every moment I wasn't at work, I found time to be with Anne. I dreaded the day she had to leave, though I knew it was inevitable. Summer would soon end, and she would have to go back home for school.

We hadn't talked religion much since that day at the hospital when she had prayed for her Aunt Bea, but Anne was very open about her faith in God. Whether words were penned or spoken, Anne wasn't afraid to say what she thought. I admired her for her faith. She was a strong person, unwavering in her trust in God. I hoped someday I could share that belief with her –I just didn't know how, and didn't know how to ask.

It had been a very hard and long day in the mint fields. Joe wanted to pinch every last ounce of oil he could from the leaves. Since this was going to be the last harvest of the season, he made sure every worker had a full day of labor. Newcomers joined his laborers to hand-pick the last crop of leaves. I finally succeeded to muddle mint the correct way in order to produce the virgin-fine mint oil. Boss Joe was very pleased with my work and kept me on the hand-press, even though he had more modern machines to do the work.

"The best oil is hand-pressed," Joe once told me. "There is no other way to get the sweetest oil. I will count on you to do it right!"

My muscles ached that night, even though I was used to the job. It turned out to be a hot, sticky, and tough day. Reminded me of the first day I learned to muddle mint many weeks before.

"Remember what happened when you crushed the leaves?" I remembered Joe's words. "Beaten oil produces a bitter taste." I had ruined the whole batch. Had to throw it away. "There will be no mistakes on this crop. You've learned your job well. You're the one I can trust to do it right. This season it will all be hand-pressed, and you're my man Frank." Joe had given me a hardy slap on my sore back that nearly took my breath away.

Muscles were so sore that night, I just wanted to go to sleep. Too tired to even see Anne, somehow dragged feet my weary bones to my room. As I entered, the setting sun seemed to make the old worn Bible on the table shine like a beacon in the darkened room. With trembling hands, I stroked the soft black leather cover. I needed a nugget tonight. Anne said the nuggets were there, just like gold. "Some words may be clear and speak into your soul, but some are more rugged and need to be pondered," she once told me. "Still other verses lay hidden to be sought after like treasure. Dig for them."

I picked up the Book. Is it true? I wondered. The old Book seemed to fall open where the purple ribbon still guarded its treasure – Mikey's and my pact. It said Isaiah 53.

"For he shall grow up before him as a tender plant..." Like the tender young mint leaf? I wondered.

"He is despised and rejected of men; a man of sorrows, and acquainted with grief... Surely he carried our sorrows...."

The words seemed to leap out: *"He carried my sorrows"*? Did that mean I could bring all my hurts and sorrows to him and he would carry them away? But there are so many – like a weight around my neck.

He was wounded – bruised – crushed. Like the mint leaf? I pondered. Why?

Lowered the old Book to the table, and placed my hand on top of it, as if willing it to guard the treasured nugget I had just uncovered. There must be more to this gem. How could I dig deeper to understand? Would have to ask Anne. She would know.

Thunder rumbled in the distance. Good. It would cool things off some. Make it easier to sleep tonight. The ground needed a gentle rain to soak the ground. The soft pitter-patter against window pane lulled me into dreamland.

I dreamt of Mac's farm. I was ten years old again feeling relief and gratefulness for a kind old grandfather-type man who took me in and cared for me like a son. Mac put his arm around my shoulder and patted it. He smiled, but the look in his eyes held warning. Somewhere behind him, the wicked witch appeared. Her hair, tied back into a thick white knot, pulled her eyes into a slanty squint. She grabbed me from Mac and started to shave my head. She forced me to eat slop from the bucket in the corner and cackled in a scary high-pitched voice that hurt my ears.

My brothers, Mike and Jesse, tried to pull me away

from her, but could not. Mikey told his invisible friend to help me. "Just ask him to help you, Frankie," Mikey said, but I argued. He pressed me into the wagon. "Just believe, Frankie." He pushed at my chest. The horse behind me pawed at the ground. Thunder boomed and a flash of light blinded my eyes.

The sky lit up as lightening streaked across the black starless expanse. The horse spooked. "You gotta believe, Frankie," yelled Mikey. My body jerked and twitched as I tried to reach the horse in my dream.

Shielded my eyes against the bright lightening in the sky. Earsplitting thunder followed a second behind, deafening my ears. The horse whinnied in fright. Rain came in torrents; I was soaked to the skin. The street became both muddy and slippery. The horse bolted, and reared back on her hind legs. Mikey ran to put himself between me and the frightened horse.

No! Mikey – don't! No. No! No!! My body jerked in spasms as the horrible scene replayed in my mind. Mikey pushed me to the ground. The terrified animal reared back again to escape the noise and light. Tried to get off the ground, but my bum leg locked up. Couldn't move. Watched the nightmare play before me like a bystander in the crowd. Couldn't scream, couldn't budge. Mikey was caught in the reins, then trampled by razor-sharp hooves. The unconscious boy was mercilessly drug through the street. The scene replayed over and over. Mikey's limp, lifeless body, tumbled over the stones like a ragdoll.

The room lit up with blinding light as another loud crack of thunder reverberated my bed. I screamed aloud and jolted upright in bed, wide awake and shaken. My body was wet from sweat; my clothes and bed were soaked from rain coming through the open window.

Shivering and cold, I sat on the edge of the bed and wept. Gut-wrenching sobs shook my body. I wasn't there for you, Mikey. You needed me, and I let you down. I cried until I could cry no more, at last releasing all my sorrows and griefs pent up so deep inside. The gruesome pain of losing my brother washed afresh through my being. The dream had been so real.

Sleep was done for tonight. Rose wearily to change my wet clothes and sheets and closed the window. I lay there for some time wide awake. Reflected on my brother. I wasn't there for him, but he had been there for me. He laid his life down for me. He died a horrendous death for his brave act. He took my place so I could live.

"Surely he hath borne our griefs, and carried our sorrows...and our peace was upon him...."

But I don't know how....Was I still dreaming? Help me. Please?

38 Reckoning

The bad storm passed and the awful nightmares with it. Needed to talk to Anne. She could explain; she would understand. We agreed to meet at church for our weekly time alone since she came back to care for Aunt Bea.

Mrs. Quincy wasn't well enough to get out and about, but she was well enough for Anne to leave the house once in a while. Church allowed us to have some quality time together, away from our responsibilities.

On the way out the door, my eyes caught sight of the large old Bible. On impulse, I picked it up and took it with me. Anne would be impressed.

We met at the door of the church and slid into a pew midway to the front. I drank in the sweet aroma of her perfume and watched the light from the stained glass make rainbows in her hair. Loved listening to Anne sing. Her voice was so sweet, so clear and pure. My sweet brown-haired angel. A warm gush of love billowed inside me. I reached over and slipped my hand around hers. She glanced at me and smiled.

Rev. Harley went to the pulpit and opened his Bible. He asked everyone to stand for the reading and turn to the scripture of the day, Isaiah 53. I looked at him in surprise. How did he know? Did God tell him? The old Bible opened immediately to the exact scripture with the purple ribbon still in its place. Anne smiled with approval and opened her Bible to follow along.

"All we like sheep have gone astray; we have turned everyone to his own way; and the LORD hath laid on him the iniquity of us all," the minister read.

Rev. Harley went on to tell the story of the sheep and how they easily lose their way without a shepherd to lead them. They can be lost forever unless someone goes to look for them.

Made me think of Mac's sheep and my work on the farm tending those stubborn sheep. I closed my eyes, nodded in agreement, and chuckled silently.

Anne gave me a slight poke in the side, "Wake up! You need to listen," she whispered with a frown that looked more like a grin.

I jumped and winked at her. Raised my eyebrows as if to say, Who? Me?

"You. Me. We are the lost sheep the scripture speaks about," the preacher continued. We are the ones who keep losing their way when we don't follow the shepherd. We end up places we never thought possible. But the Good Shepherd will go anywhere to find the one lost lamb to bring him back to the fold."

Nodded again. Yep. That was true. Recalled the many times spent looking for one stubborn sheep that refused to stay with the flock. Always seemed like the same one. It insisted on going its own way. Sort of like me, I mused – gone my own way most of my years. Had to. Never accepted much advice from anyone, except for Mr. Neiman and perhaps Mrs. Quincy, and of course from Anne.

"Jesus said, '*I am the Good Shepherd who came to lay down his life for his sheep.*' He was bruised and beaten, broken, and then murdered just for you and me. He did it so we could find our way back to the fold again," the reverend preached. "God wants you to find your way again; to be at peace with yourself and with God."

Shifted in my seat and fumbled with the Bible pages. Felt like his words were pointed right at me. Had Anne told Rev. Harley about my circumstances? But she couldn't have. How could he have known the horrible nightmares I had just last night? How did he know I begged God for peace? A big lump formed in my throat. Felt like I would choke. The room was cool, but I was hot. Beads of sweat formed on my forehead. Felt my body tremble. Desperate for peace – scared inside. Wanted to run; felt the need to escape, but something held me on the pew. I twitched and wiggled in my seat.

Anne shot me a motherly frown. "You okay?" she whispered in my ear.

I nodded and tried to smile, but it was forced and she noticed. Felt trapped; had to get out of there. Tried to change my position, and as I did, the old Bible began to slip from my lap. Caught it just before it hit the floor, but the yellowed piece of paper escaped the thin pages and floated to the floor. Both Anne and I reached for it at the same time. She picked it up, opened it, and together we read Mikey's and my pact in silence: "*We promise to always be there for each other and never leave one another in danger. Signed Mikey and Frankie.*

The huge lump grew in my throat. I choked away the inevitable tears and squeezed my eyes tight so they wouldn't spill out. I fingered the old blood prints of our pact. My heart thumped hard. As if he heard my unspoken thoughts, the preacher answered.

"God knows your thoughts; he knows your heart. He hears your questions and sees your anxiety. He's here today to bring you peace and direction for your life. You can take Him home with you today, if you only ask..."

Just ask. Just believe. Those were Mikey's words.

Anne grabbed my hand and squeezed tight. She sensed my discomfort and conviction. I squeezed back, but did not dare look at her. If I opened my eyes, all my bottled-up tears would spill out.

A solo voice began to sing, "*I surrender all; I surrender all.*"

The preacher spoke again, "God will always be there for you; He will be there when no one else is. He is closer than a brother, and He is ready to help you find your way home. He will never leave you nor forsake you. Are you ready today to give Him a chance in your life?"

It was like a light went on. Everything suddenly became crystal clear. Mikey laid down his life for mine. He did it willingly, with no thought for his own safety. I should have been the one who died. God's son, Jesus, laid down his life for me too, for my eternal life. I didn't deserve this love or his favor, yet he was willing to give it. Took a huge breath and let it escape from my lungs long and slow. Yes. I was ready to find that peace. I needed to find the way to real life. I needed to come home. I will surrender it all – my past, my present, my future.

Guess my journey started the night before during the storm. Or maybe, it started years ago and I just didn't know it. But now my heart was ready. I squeezed Anne's hand tighter and searched her beautiful brown eyes with hot tears in mine.

"Will you go up with me?" I whispered.

C.A. SIMONSON

39 Birth Day

That Sunday began a whole new chapter in my life. It forever changed me. I found a new life and peace never known before. My soul felt so full, so clean. It seemed it would burst from the inside out! I wished my sisters and oldest brother could know the wonderful freshness my heart felt, as if every weight had been lifted from a lifetime of sorrow. If only I knew where they were, I could tell them. Most of all, I wished Mikey and Jesse could know. Somehow deep down in my heart, I believed they already knew and smiled their approval from heaven.

"Aunt Bea has improved so much," Anne informed me one night at dinner. "She's able to get up and about a lot more and do things on her own. The doctor says she won't need any help soon."

"That's good!" I nodded. God had answered my prayer for Ms. Q even though it was simple from someone who didn't know how to pray.

"So, she won't need me around to care for her much longer. The nurse will still come once a week to check on her, but she doesn't need someone here every day and night now."

"What do you mean?" My face turned to a frown.

"You know, silly. School starts the first of next month. I need to return home and get ready." Anne looked intently into my eyes. I gave her an "I-don't-get-it" look. She put her arms around my neck and squeezed. "I wish you could come with me, Frank."

I buried my face in her jasmine-scented hair and hugged her, but didn't say anything. Her words caught me off guard. Guess she did have to go back to school, but it hadn't crossed my mind. Couldn't imagine how it would be with her gone. I liked her here; enjoyed sharing time with my angel. I didn't speak, but held on tight.

Anne was good at sensing my mood. She pushed away from my hold and locked her eyes on mine. "What's wrong, Frankie?" she cooed, stroking my face in her hands. "You going to miss me?"

"Just wish you didn't have to go. Kind of like you here – with me." I pulled her in close again and kissed her forehead.

She patted my cheeks playfully and gave me her sweet ruby smile.

"Me too," she giggled, "now let me go! I have to clear the table."

She stacked the plates, gave me a wink and waltzed toward the kitchen. Then just as quick, she turned around and plopped the dishes back on the table.

"Frank!" She fluttered her eyelids. Her eyes brightened as the idea popped into her head. "Let's do something special this weekend. Want to?"

"Like what?"

"Like..." she tapped her finger to her chin, "...like go on a picnic. Okay, Frank?" She slipped her hands around my neck again and gazed into my eyes.

My heart melted, but I tried to act aloof. "Why?" I teased.

"To celebrate your birthday!" She poked at my check.

"You're teasing me now, funny girl." I laughed. "My birthday is way past. It was in July."

"Really?" she sing-songed, her eyes flirted.

"Yeah. Besides, you know I don't celebrate birthdays."

"Oh, you do now, Mr. Frank. You have a new birthday to celebrate, and I am going to plan something great! It will be real special – you'll see. She giggled, flung her hair over her shoulder, and whirled around.

I loved this girl – her enthusiasm, her spunk, her love for life. Anne embraced life with every ounce of her being. I couldn't resist her charms.

"What do you mean, new birthday?"

"You get to celebrate the day you became a new person, Frank! *The old man has gone away and all things have become new!*" That's what the Bible says. God has given you a "New Birth" day! I'll even make a cake! So what do you say? Can we go on a picnic – right after church – just you and me?"

"Just you and me?" I winked and teased.

"Just you and me, Frankie-dear."

C.A. SIMONSON

40 New Life – New Love

Sunday morning arrived with dark clouds in the sky and ominous rumbles in the distance. I feared Anne's plans for a picnic would be spoiled by a late summer downpour. It started to sprinkle as I entered the church. Anne saw me and motioned to me, patting the empty seat beside her.

"I think it's going to rain, missy," I whispered as I slid in beside her.

"It will pass – you'll see," she said with a knowing smile. "I asked God to give us a beautiful day with lots of sunshine."

I smiled inside and thanked God for my optimist angel, always positive and upbeat; she always looked for the one bright spot to shine through.

"I hope you're right. I'll put in a word, too," I grinned.

The service proceeded as usual. We sang hymns and the preacher preached. This Sunday seemed so much different though; everything seemed alive and fresh for the first time, like I had new ears. Pastor Harley spoke about giving service to the King, like a soldier who serves for justice and honor. I liked that idea. It made sense. It made me want to do whatever I could to assist others who needed help. Now I understood why Anne was so passionate about helping her aunt give away food baskets, or offering help whenever asked. She was doing it for her King. I made up my mind to talk to the pastor about this. Surely there was something I could do. I wanted to see where I fit. Excitement flooded my heart as I pondered his words.

My revelry was broken by the loud "Amen!" from the man behind me. Service was over. Bright beams of sun streamed through the stained glass windows and bounced off the floors. Anne's prayer had indeed been answered. The rain was gone, and the air gave off a sweet, clean scent mixed with the sweet perfume of autumn flowers. Bright sun and blue skies heightened both our senses and our spirits as we left the church. It was going to be a grand day together.

With no clue to what Anne had planned, she suggested we bring a change of clothes. She told me to drive west from town and she would give directions as we drove. My curiosity was piqued.

"Where are you taking me, my lady?"

"Oh – somewhere special, my prince. Just a few more miles now."

After driving a couple minutes in silence, Anne broached a delicate subject in my soul.

"I'm so proud of you, Frank!" She squeezed my arm and snuggled up close to me in the driver's seat. "But I have a question to ask you."

"Sure, anything."

"Well, that little piece of paper – the one that fell from your Bible today?"

"Ummm, yeah?"

"Well, would you tell me about it? Mikey was your

brother, right? The one who always told you about Jesus?

"Yeah."

"Can you tell me what happened to him?"

Her warm gaze of love and concern made my heart skip a beat. How could I refuse? How could I hold back any secret from her? I began to tell her the story of how our family became separated, and each one went their own way.

"So you found Mikey again when you were twelve?"

"Yep. Almost two years after we parted ways. Found out Mikey and Jesse only lived a couple miles away."

"And how old was he when he..."

"Mikey was almost eleven when he was killed..." My chest heaved as a big sigh escaped. "...when he laid down his life for mine." I was surprised. Though sad, the memory didn't sting as bad as it used to. "He threw himself in front of me, and was trampled to death. For a long time I was so mad at God. I blamed him for taking both my brothers from me. Believed he was a cruel God, not a loving one. Harsh and mean, like a lot of other people I've known in my life."

"I'm sorry, Frank," Anne stroked my arm and laid her head on my shoulder.

"He's in heaven now, I'm sure of it. He still has my back. He's still there for me – in a strange kind of up-there way."

"Yes, I know he is too." Anne sat quiet a minute. "Frankie?"

"Yeah?"

"What about your sisters, and Guy, your big brother?"

"I don't know where they are. When we parted ways, that was it. Never expected to see them again."

"But, don't you wonder?"

"Well, sure I wonder, but what can I do?"

"Maybe you should go back."

"What do you mean, go back?"

"Go back to your hometown – to Tekamah. See if anyone knows about them or where they went."

"I swore I would never go back, Annie."

"But, you said yourself – Mikey and Jesse only lived two miles away, and you didn't know it for almost two years. Maybe the girls live close by too. You need to go. You need to find out for yourself. They are your family."

"Oh, Anne. My dear, sweet Anne. You really don't know what you ask." I shook my head.

"Well, promise me you'll think about it, okay? And pray about it too," she added. "It will help you complete your journey into a new life."

I put my arm around her, pulled her closer to me, and gave her a squeeze. The rest of the drive was quiet as she gave me time to think.

"Next turn, Frank. We're almost there."

We pulled into a little park area along the road where a little creek bubbled as it wound its way into the woods. Trails beckoned guests to venture among huge maple and cottonwood trees with flowers of every kind blooming throughout the park. She led me to a quiet, out-of-the-way area, and we spread the blanket on the ground under a grand oak. We decided to walk the trail before we ate our picnic lunch. Hands interlocked, we walked in silence a long ways before any words were spoken. Words were not needed; being together was enough.

Anne was buoyant. I loved how her ponytail bounced as she walked. Reminded me of the first day I met her. Her cheeks flushed pink and her flirtatious brown eyes sparkled with excitement and mystery. The spark in my heart grew to a blaze. I fell in love with her with fresh new reality. She would head north for home in the big city at the end of the week. I had to let her know how I felt before she left. I had waited too long already. We settled on to the blanket for our picnic lunch.

"Anne..." I tilted her chin, "I have been thinking."

"That's a start," she teased, "but it sounds dangerous." She shoved a chicken leg in my mouth and forced me to take a bite. "Here, have some chicken." She began to laugh so hard she held her sides. Her laughter was contagious.

"You're so much fun, Frank! I will truly miss you." She aimed a carrot stick at my nose and jumped up before I could react. "Oh yeah – that reminds me. Wait there!" she yelled behind her back as she ran back to the truck.

What a lucky guy I am to have a girl like her. No— it is more than luck. God sent her to me; she's my very own angel. I must tell her.

And, maybe she is right. Maybe I should go back to Tekamah one more time. Settle things and move on. I determined then and there a trip was in my future. Though I wanted Anne to go with me, that would not happen. This would have to be done alone. This was my journey to complete.

She returned a couple minutes later with her hands behind her back. She pulled out a small, wrapped, rectangular package to give me a peek, then hid it behind her again.

"You want it?" she taunted. She held the package toward me, then as I reached up for it, she snatched it behind her again. After a couple tries, I raised up on my hands and knees and grabbed at her like a wild man. Anne wrinkled up her quirky little nose and let out a delightful squeal.

"You want it, Mr. Frank? Come and get it!" she giggled again and took off on a sprint like a little girl again, holding the package high above her head. "Bet you can't catch me, Frankie-boy!"

Jumped up and took off after her —around bushes, behind trees, dodging this way and that. It didn't take long to catch up to her; she wanted to be caught.

Took a leap, wrapped my arms around her, and we both tumbled to the ground, gasping for breath. The roughed-up package flew from her hand and ripped open. We lay on the ground laughing and panting hard from the chase. She stared into the beautiful blue sky with all its white, fluffy clouds.

"It was supposed to rain today," she said. "And just look. Not a single rain cloud up there." The marvel was heard in her voice. "God is so good to us." She smiled and kissed my cheek, then rolled out of my embrace to retrieve the tattered package.

"Here, Frank. A present for you." She handed the tattered bundle to me. "It's for your "new birth" day." I could tell without even opening it that it was a special book.

"A Bible? Anne, you got me a Bible?"

"Yes. It's very special to me. Now it's your very own Bible, Frank. Something to start your new birth off right. It's your guide book, your prayer book, your treasure map. I hope you don't think that sounds dumb. I wanted you to have something to help us stay close when I leave. Something to remember me by. If anything will do that, it's this Book."

"But Anne, this is your Bible."

"I have other Bibles. I want you to have this one. If you keep this, you will keep a part of me. I want to share this part of me with you. It has all my notes in it Frank – the treasures I have found. There are notes about you too. Read it, and you will discover more truth and learn from one who can always give you direction."

Her soft eyes had the look of love and devotion and she implored my approval. I nodded my appreciation with a smile, and a large heart of thankfulness.

"It's priceless, Anne. I will treasure it with all my heart. There's only one thing that would make me happier..." I paused to stroke her hair and look into her beautiful, sweet face.

"Go on, Frank!" she insisted. "What would make you happier?"

I wrapped her in my arms and held her close. "You. You, Anne. I want you."

She didn't seem a bit surprised. She let out a huge sigh, and cuddled into my arms. Her body felt warm against mine. She didn't say anything, only blushed a beautiful pink.

"I love you Anne. From the first day I saw you, I've loved you. You've helped me so much. You've lived a pure life before me, and taught me about the only One who could grant me peace and real life. You are my special angel from God. I don't know how I can live without you. Will you be mine, Anne? Will you be my angel forever?"

She wrapped her arms around my neck. Her lips met mine for the first and sweetest kiss of my lifetime.

"I love you too, Frank —and yes, if my Lord wills, I'll be yours forever."

ABOUT THE AUTHOR

C. A. Simonson is a writer, author, editor, , and graphic artist. She has over 200 publications – fiction and nonfiction – in anthologies, magazine articles, newspaper articles, and other tabloids.
She has served on the board of the Springfield Writer's Guild in Missouri and is also a member of Columbia Writers' Guild. She is the mother of two sons and grandmother to six grandchildren. She lives in the country near Strafford, Missouri where she enjoys fishing and gardening.

I hope you enjoyed reading *Love's Journey Home.* Look for the sequel *Love Looks Back: The Search for Siblings* coming soon.

Friend me on Facebook:
https://www.facebook.com/CASimonsonBooks
Follow me on Twitter:
https://twitter.com/candysimonson
Connect on LinkedIn:
www.linkedin.com/pub/candace-simonson

Subscribe to my blogs at: http://casimonson.wordpress.com
http://kitchentipsandtreasures.wordpress.com

Your pen is your sword.
Wield it wisely, for it is a weapon of truth.

Made in the USA
Middletown, DE
24 September 2022